GOD'S DEVIL

GOD'S DEVIL

&

OTHER TALES TO WHET
THE THEOLOGICAL
IMAGINATION

JOHN WARWICK MONTGOMERY

God's Devil: And Other Tales To Whet the Theological Imagination

© 2020 New Reformation Publications

All rights reserved. No part of this publication may be reproduced, distributed, or transmitted in any form or by any means, including photocopying, recording, or other electronic or mechanical methods, without the prior written permission of the publisher, except in the case of brief quotations embodied in critical reviews and certain other noncommercial uses permitted by copyright law. For permission requests, write to the publisher at the address below.

Scriptures are taken from the King James Version (KJV): King James Version, public domain.

Published by:
1517 Publishing
PO Box 54032
Irvine, CA 92619-4032

Publisher's Cataloging-In-Publication Data
(Prepared by The Donohue Group, Inc.)

Names: Montgomery, John Warwick, author. | Egoshina, Vera, illustrator.
Title: God's devil : and other tales to whet the theological imagination / John Warwick Montgomery ; story illustrations by Vera Egoshina.
Description: Irvine, CA : 1517 Publishing, [2020]
Identifiers: ISBN 9781948969505 (case laminate) | ISBN 9781948969376 (paperback) | ISBN 9781948969383 (ebook)
Subjects: LCSH: Theology—Fiction. | LCGFT: Short stories.
Classification: LCC PS3613.O54861 G63 2020 (print) | LCC PS3613.O54861 (ebook) | DDC 813./6—dc23

Printed in the United States of America

Cover art by Brenton Clarke Little

For

Craig and Ellen Parton

and

Dallas & Marjorie Miller

who love a good story

Contents

Preface ix

God's Devil: A Ghost Story with a Moral 1

The Search for Ultimates:
A Sherlockian Inquiry 47

A Royal Visit 95

Judgment Eve 107

Preface

The stories comprising this little book span more than half a century.

First in time is "God's Devil: A Ghost Story with a Moral," which first appeared in a *Chiaroscuro*, a Canadian literary magazine (4, 1961), and was later reprinted as a chapter in the author's *Principalities and Powers: The World of the Occult*.

Next came "The Search for Ultimates: A Sherlockian Inquiry" in 1993. The story was first presented as a university lecture in California (to the irritation of some attending philosophers, who wanted something secular, dull, and incomprehensible). Publication, together with other Holmesian essays of mine eventually took place: *The Transcendent*

Holmes (Ashcroft, British Columbia: Calabash Press, 2000).

"A Royal Visit" came to be written as a result of my long-term fascination with the Magi in Matthew's narrative of our Lord's birth—and my infuriation with efforts (even by some evangelical scholars) to reduce that biblical material to Midrash level. If you want historical fact, go to Matthew; if you prefer fiction that makes theological points, read the third chapter of the present book! (Not so incidentally, for a comprehensive bibliographical treatment of the Magi traditions, go to Hugo Kehrer, *Die Heiligen Drei Könige in Literatur und Kunst* [2 vols.; Leipzig: E. A. Seemann, 1908–9].)

Our final story, "Judgment Eve," grew out of my contacts with a wide swath of orthodox, pseudo-orthodox, and outrightly heretical folk over the years whose theologies—as the adage puts it—"if converted into hair, would not make a wig for a grape." What would be the reaction of the Judge of Heaven and Earth to such notions?

"A Royal Visit" and "Judgment Eve" are published here for the first time.

The author trusts that readers will enjoy—and gain something religiously substantial—from these little samples of theology disguised as fiction.

> John Warwick Montgomery
> 15th June 2020
> The Feast Day of St. Vitus

God's Devil

A GHOST STORY WITH A MORAL

Though Bishop Pike was wrong (as usual) in wanting the Creed to be sung but not said, certain truths can be conveyed more effectively in parable or story than in ordinary propositional discourse. Especially is this true of the supernatural realms of Faerie, and even more so of the dark borderlands of occult evil. Indeed, someone has suggested that Dante's Inferno *is the most effective unit of the* Divine Comedy *because, in describing the nether regions, he speaks so fully from his own experience! Whether my tale should be taken as exemplifying that truth is a moot question (though there are genuine autobiographical details embedded there—I leave to the reader the task of winnowing them). No apologies are in order for the moral quality of the story, for ghost*

The demons Astaroth, Eurynome; Baël, Amduscias; and Belphegor, Asmodeus (from Collin de Plancy's *Dictionnaire infernal*, Paris, 1863)

stories are invariably (perhaps inevitably) moralistic: one can hardly bump up against "heaven and its wonders and hell" without having to face one's own relationship to them and to the spectral haunts of earth. So with appreciation for the chills I have received from Le Fanu, M. R. James, John Buchan, and a host of others, most of whom are now themselves shades, here is the tale.[1]

"So you actually did it. You've become a damned bible-toting clergyman." The smile on Cavender's face was compounded roughly of sixty percent cynicism and forty percent genuine interest; knowing from my college days that one could almost never expect a better ratio from him, I realized that no insult was intended. Here, in the hubbub of meaningless small talk which seemed to be moving toward absurdity but never quite reaching it, he wanted a satisfying conversational exchange perhaps as much as I did.

We were standing in front of the large fireplace with the gothic inscription staring out at us as it had so frequently when we were at school together:

---

1. Originally published in *Chiaroscuro*, 4 (1961).

Ah life! The mere living! How fit to employ all the heart and the soul and the mind forever in joy!

"How appropriate," I thought to myself. "Since Cavender and I graduated from old Cornell ten years ago, we have both managed to live out Willard Straight's rather banal aphorism—as long as different definitions of 'joy' are permitted."

"Yes," I said, laughing. "I've become a clergyman—and I'll even accept the adjective 'damned,' since a cleric doesn't escape being *simul justus et peccator*."

"'Saint and sinner at the same time,' eh? Good God, you're not just a cleric, you're a theologian to boot." Cavender's face now registered real surprise and a trace of something vaguely approaching admiration. "Notice that your Latin didn't snow me. Old hellfire Luther, right? Three cheers for my classical education—it finally seems to be paying off in polite conversation as well as in my authority-conscious profession."

"The law, of course," I replied. "You were moving in that direction in your senior year. And"—I eyed my profane friend to see his reaction—"a caustic wit like yours would go to waste outside of dramatic courtroom situations."

"Quite so, quite so," Cavender said, laughing. "And a corporation mouthpiece at that. But why I ended up peeking under Justice's blindfold is the usual drab tale. Whyte's organization man, Riesman's other-directed American, and a wee bit of Oliver Wendell Holmes—put them all together and they don't spell 'mother,' they spell 'Ross Cavender.' But what I want to know is why you ended up with your intellectual and sartorial collars on backward. *That* should be worth hearing. I presume that like George Fox you heard the 'call' and now you spend your spare moments walking barefoot and yelling, 'Woe, woe to the bloody city of Lichfield'—or rather—'New York.' Come on, let's get the hell out of this highball-jiggling madhouse and you can tell me about it."

Without waiting for a reply, Cavender started for the door of the Great Hall. His voice trailed off as he elbowed his rather stocky frame through the Amy Vanderbilt–ish crowd:

"Why in thunder does any sane man come to an alumni reunion? Did all these bastards actually graduate . . ."

I followed as best I could, though not with quite the Cavender aplomb. He headed for the wainscoted browsing-library. Apparently the alumni had not lost the antipathy to scholarly literature which four years of university education manages to create: the library was practically deserted. We sat down in the far corner near the roaring wood fire. Cavender grabbed an ashtray and lit another cigarette from the one he was just finishing. I took out my pipe.

"So," I said, "You want me to tell you how I came to enter the ministry—how I became interested in theology. Actually these are two questions, not one. You remember that in college I was something of a do-gooder—causes, etc. Probably that would have been enough to put me in clerical garb; it certainly landed me in theological seminary. But as to how I got the *intellectual* collar on backward—that's a different story. That happened *in* seminary, not before."

"Oh, no!" Cavender broke in. "Am I going to hear the fascinating story of how Theology 650 opened your eyes to—what's the Swedenborgian phrase—'heaven and its wonders and hell'? In a sense, I suppose

I asked for it. But please, don't get too emotional; I have a sympathetic ulcer."

"Relax, Ross," I answered. "It isn't going to be that kind of tale."

"I hope not. And spare the academic minutiae. My LLB was no snap, you know. Even today, the very thought of the supersedeas writ makes my blood run cold."

"It's odd that you should speak of blood running cold," I said. "That definitely ties in with a certain event in my seminary experience—an event I was about to describe to you. As a result of it, I became—how shall I put it?—theologically inclined. And maybe without it, I would never have finished seminary or been ordained. Shall I go on?"

"Sure, sure. As I said, asked for it. I'll try not to derail your train of thought again."

The fire was burning brightly: the few people who had been in the room when we entered were now gone. The cocktail hour had passed, and the winter evening was already settling down around us. With the realization that I could have told the story only to a skeptic such as Cavender—since his ridicule was predictable—I began.

• • •

Theological seminary is an unpleasant period for many who go through it. I think this was doubly so for me. There was the usual feeling of intellectual descent, for, say what you will about a secular university, heat is seldom substituted for light there. But over and above that, I felt definite alienation from the whole program. What did all this doctrine and biblical study have to do with *life* and with changing society? In college, I had been what C. S. Lewis somewhere calls a "Christianity-and" man—"Christianity-and-pacifism," "Christianity-and-vegetarianism," etc. I wanted to set the world right-side up. Marx turned Hegel's dialectic on its head; I wanted to put corrupt America—or some segment of it—on its feet again. But what good was abstract doctrine? "Justification by grace through faith": I thought it was utterly impractical. "The resurrection": absurd and irrelevant. "The new birth": revolting. "Angelology and demonology": medieval and essentially immoral. It was my middler year in seminary, and I had just about decided to quit the whole business. For the previous week, I had been reading and comparing catalogs of schools of social work. No pie-in-the-sky idealism there!

Then I received my preaching assignment to St. Paul's church on the Old Drummer's Road.

Perhaps I had better explain the expression "preaching assignment." (*At this point, Cavender mumbled that he didn't care much one way or the other—but if it would make me happy . . .*) At the small seminaries of our denomination, the students are expected to lead the services at nearby churches with vacant pulpits. The theory is that the student can't do excessive harm to the congregation, and the congregational experience may conceivably do the student some good psychologically. Moreover, at least in my seminary situation, the experience definitely did the congregations and the students good financially, since, on the one hand, the pulpits could be filled at fees so ridiculously low that an ordained man would not even consider them sufficient for carfare, and, on the other, the students were generally so broke that any remuneration was viewed as manna from heaven.

Since I was unquestionably in the latter category (this being, I felt, my only genuine common ground with the other students), I leaped at the chance to take the assignment.

I should mention that our seminary was in one of the older rural sections of the Midwest. Little towns connected by irrationally laid-out roads dotted the whole area in a radius of three hundred miles around the seminary. A file of old church bulletins and maps drawn by previous student pastors was the best way of keeping track of the numerous churches which begged for aid—in the most heartrending terms—from time to time.

After the assignment came from elderly Dean Rylsford ("Bless his heart," I thought, "The seminary would disintegrate without him"), I consulted the file. I went through it three times, looking under "P" for "Paul's," "S" for "Saint," and finally—cursing (but just "damn," for this isn't really "taking the name of the Lord thy God in vain")—under "I" for "Indiana." Nothing. Then I took all the files out of the battered desk drawer and found, crumpled at the back, an old map telling how to get to St. Paul's. The paper was badly yellowed, and the writing was almost illegible. The map had apparently been held too near a fire on some occasion, for it was plainly scorched. But it gave me the directions I needed, and that was all I cared.

Sunday morning, I arose early—but no earlier than absolutely necessary. When faced with a preaching assignment, my regular procedure was to determine the exact distance to the church, divide it by forty miles an hour (the average speed my car could travel without the motor dropping out), add one half hour for service preliminaries at the church, and then get up not a minute before the required time. Since St. Paul's appeared from the map to be one hundred and twenty miles away, and the service was scheduled for ten thirty, I left the seminary at seven.

It was a stormy February day—the first Sunday in Lent, to be exact. Wisps of snow were in the air, and the wind was strong. Fortunately, the roads were clear; I would make good time.

The first lap of the journey was along Highway 37, a well-paved east-west road crossing the state. I was to go eighty miles due west before turning off onto a county road. I felt relieved that the first part of the trip was to be so unproblematic. I would have an opportunity to run through my sermon again. The speedometer registered exactly forty.

My sermon was on the Gospel lesson for the day, and if I did say so myself, it was one of my better homiletic creations. A year before, when I first delivered it on a similar preaching assignment, it had gone over very well. I still remembered the wife of a member of the church council saying at the door after the service, "You have a great future ahead of you, young man." Perhaps she was right, but I was no longer sure that it lay in the ordained ministry. Thank goodness this was a Sunday when I could give one of my really satisfying sermons; I didn't think I could have stomached again, for example, the naïve, supernaturalistic message I had once prepared for the previous Sunday of the church year when the Gospel lesson reads:

> Then He took unto Him the twelve, and said unto them, Behold, we go up to Jerusalem, and all things that are written by the prophets concerning the Son of man shall be accomplished. For He shall be delivered unto the Gentiles, and shall be mocked, and spitefully entreated, and spitted on: and they shall scourge Him, and put Him to death: and the third day He shall rise again. (Luke 18:31–33)

I had certainly beat the drum for fulfilled prophecy and a historical resurrection in that sermon! How simpleminded can one be? And I had noticed that the comments at the church door afterward were not at all as effusive as I would have liked. Some people even had tears in their eyes.

But this Sunday would be different. It is true that on the surface, the Gospel lesson seemed typically theological and miraculously orientated. But it just needed the kind of modern interpretation my sermon provided. You, of course, remember that Gospel lesson for the first Sunday in Lent. (*"Naturally," Cavender said with a sly smile, "but you might refresh my memory on the details."*)

The lesson is the familiar temptation-in-the-wilderness passage, beginning, "Then was Jesus led up of the Spirit into the wilderness to be tempted of the devil." The old devil presents three temptations: make stones into bread to satisfy hunger, do a miracle to show personal power, and worship evil in order to obtain all the kingdoms of the world. Naturally, Jesus refuses. Sounds a bit histrionic and overdone as it stands, eh? That's what I thought, and in my sermon, I attempted to bring out the *real* essence of the passage.

First, I pointed out that the modern mind has to give up the primitive idea of a personal evil being ("devil," "Satan," etc.). However, as a symbol, the concept still has meaning, for it indicates how far short of evolutionary perfection we still are. (The previous year, some of the congregation had appeared puzzled at the phrase "evolutionary perfection," but I determined to retain it, for it's a compliment to a congregation to speak over its head on occasion.) Then I dealt with the temptations themselves. What was the point of them all? Why, to show the evils of selfishness. If Jesus had made the stones into bread for *others*—if he had jumped off the pinnacle of the temple in an attempt to show others that society should learn to control the powers of nature, if he had gained the kingdoms of the world in order to create a model government and social milieu for the benefit of mankind— "then," I had thundered a year before, "then the situation would have been different, far different." This passage, I argued, should warn all of us against the dangers of self-centered lives, and we should follow Jesus, the ideal Master, in rejecting all temptation to do ourselves good when we should be doing good for others.

The sermon sounded even better to me as I reviewed it than it had a year before, and I particularly prided myself that I had exactly countered the advice of my drab homiletics professor "to present Jesus always as Savior, never merely as example." But further musing was now impossible, for I had reached the turnoff.

The map told me to go left—that is, south—on County Route 6A and continue on for twenty miles until I reached Sodom Junction. The road was not very well paved, and the wind was definitely increasing in velocity. It was already nine thirty; apparently, I had let the speed drop below forty miles an hour while I was going over the sermon. Now I had to concentrate entirely on the driving or I would be late. This thought made my stomach turn over, for Dean Rylsford, though a mild man, had one phobia: students must not be late for assigned services. Of course, what difference did it make if I were going to leave seminary anyway? But, I reproached myself, even the philosopher Kant maintained such a regular schedule that the burghers of Konigsberg could set their clocks by his walks to and from the university. I pressed harder on the accelerator.

At five minutes before ten, I arrived at Sodom Junction—if such a collection of ramshackle old stores and deteriorating houses could be dignified by a name. Why it was called a "junction" I could not imagine, for there were no train tracks that I could see. But the "Sodom" was certainly appropriate, I said to myself—if one thought of the biblical Sodom after, and not before, the fire descended from heaven (or rather, I rationally corrected myself, natural volcanic eruption engulfed it).

I was now to turn right on the dirt road which crossed 6A. This was called the Old Drummer's Road, according to the map, and St. Paul's church was on a cutoff some twenty miles beyond Sodom Junction. I tried to see a road sign or directional indicator for confirmation, but there was neither. Since it was Sunday morning, the stores were all closed and even the houses showed no sign of life. "Probably damned superstitious Catholics," I thought, "up for six a.m. mass and now back in bed." However, there could be little real doubt about the route, for only one east-west road crossed 6A at the town. I wheeled the car to the right and started off again. Ten o'clock—just a half hour to go. By my original schedule, I should have arrived at the church by now.

I gunned the motor, and in spite of the wretched driving conditions—snow was now coming down steadily, and the wind was blowing it directly at the windshield—I managed to maintain an insane speed of fifty-five. Fifteen minutes went by. I was becoming more and more nervous.

The road began to twist and turn. The landscape (as much as I could see of it) became heavily wooded but had a burned-over appearance.

At 10:25, to my great relief, I saw the church, just off the road to my left.

It was a profoundly depressing sight—more depressing, if possible, than Sodom Junction. The building was short and squat, and though built in a cruciform pattern, the transepts were far longer than the nave. Obviously, the builders had had only a rough idea of proper ecclesiastical symbolism. The exterior was of brick and was blackened from age or perhaps from a fire which had given the woods their burned appearance, but which had been stopped just before it reached the church.

There was no parking area, and no other cars were visible. I pulled over to the left side of the narrow road, switched off the motor, yanked the emergency brake on, and leaped out of the car.

As I did so, the wooden double doors of the church opened (they were a sickly yellow-orange color—perhaps they had originally been an off-shade of red), and a man of about seventy appeared. He moved stiffly and slowly down the steps and came toward me. His bent frame reminded me of a large bug, but that, I said to myself, was hardly the gracious thought a seminarian should have toward one of God's old soldiers.

"You must be our young man from N— Seminary," he wheezed. "You had us a bit worried, though we seldom start the services right on time. My name is Oldstone—Enoch Oldstone—and I am president of the council. Do come in out of the damp."

I followed him into the church while exchanging the usual pleasantries. The interior was one of the strangest I had ever encountered—and I had seen many examples of midwestern churchmanship.

The strangeness did not come from any bizarre substitutions for the usual appointments, such as in one little Ohio congregation where I had been appalled to find colored Christmas tree lights used on the altar throughout the year. Rather, one received the impression in St. Paul's that everything was almost correct, but not quite. For one thing, in line with the squat exterior of the building, the horizontal dimension seemed to predominate over the vertical: the pulpit was too low, the altar was too low, the candles on it were too short. And the cross—the altar cross—could its horizontal axis possibly be longer than the vertical? Clearly it was a Greek cross and not a Latin one; there was nothing wrong with that, needless to say, but the vertical axis did look shorter. Perhaps it was an illusion due to the bad lighting, I told myself. The stained-glass windows were competently done but in much too somber shades. Almost Calvinistic in their severity, I thought. And the scenes! What odd choice had dictated them? Oh, they were biblical all right, but they depicted such Old Testament episodes as Saul consulting the witch of Endor and Elisha's bears eating the insolent children, and such New Testament events as Ananias and Sapphira being struck dead and Simon Magus attempting to buy the Holy Spirit. My eyes traveled to the congregation itself, if it could be called such. There were not more than twenty-five people present in all, though the church could have held ten times that number. They were not seated together, but (I thought with relief) at least they sat near the chancel. Then I saw the reason: an old wood-burning stove not far from the pulpit. And yet it was certainly warm enough in here without sitting that close to the stove . . .

I suddenly realized that Enoch Oldstone had asked me a question. Flustered, I had to have it repeated.

"Would you like to have me go over the peculiarities of our service with you, young man?" he queried in a rasping voice.

"I don't think that will be necessary, thank you," I replied. "I have done a great deal of supply preaching in recent years." (The plural "years" was a bit of an exaggeration, but I liked to set nervous congregational members at ease.) "You might, however, mention any radical differences between your service and the Common Service."

"Well," he began with a hoarse chuckle which I did not entirely like, "we have made a few alterations—but what congregation hasn't, I always say. Every congregation has its favorite portions of the service, and traditions do grow up. Doesn't the Confession put it well when it says, 'It is not necessary that rites and ceremonies everywhere be the same'?"

I nodded painfully, wondering what was coming next. I had never been especially good at introducing liturgical innovations without prior practice.

Apparently sensing my dismay, Oldstone said, "My boy, why not just let me take the opening liturgy? I serve as lay reader here regularly, and"—he gave me an odd look out of the corner of his eye—"we don't get young men of your potential very often. We want to make you feel at home, yes, right at home." (Why did he stress that? I asked myself.) "You just give the sermon. It is on the Gospel lesson, isn't it?"

I nodded.

"Wonderful!" He clasped his thin hands together. "A glorious passage! It's our favorite here at St. Paul's, or as we familiarly call our old church, St. 'Pollyon's. The ending seems a bit inconclusive, but"—he added hastily—"we shouldn't question things deeper than ourselves. As the Good Book says, 'His ways are deeper than our ways.'"

I was sure that the verse read "higher" rather than "deeper," but there was no point in being pedantic. I accepted the offer with great relief.

By then, an old lady had begun to play the prelude on the pedal organ. A deep depression was settling over me as we walked slowly up the aisle and took our seats. I was so overwhelmed, either from the exhaustion of driving or from the excessive heat in the chancel, that I fancied the prelude to consist of selections from Wagner's *Götterdämmerung*. "What absurdity," I thought. "I must get a hold on myself before the sermon."

Oldstone carried the liturgy along very effectively, I had to admit. But he mumbled to such an extent that I found it difficult to catch the words. At a few points, he seemed to become positively elated, as for example at the Introit and the Gradual when the Psalm reads, "He that dwelleth in the secret place of the Most High." The Gloria Patri and the Gloria in Excelsis did not, as far as I could determine, come into the service at all, but this was probably one of the local variations Oldstone had referred to previously. The Creed plainly had been reworked, and the phrase "principalities and powers" was inserted at several places. But my mind was badly muddled. I could not be certain what was said. The heat was becoming insufferable.

Finally the time for the sermon arrived. I rose and went to the pulpit. Oldstone jumped up ahead of me and removed a worn volume from it to make room for my notes. Did I read the title right as "Malleus maleficarum"?

I looked out at the twenty-five or so men and women in front of me. Their eyes, I realized with suppressed horror, were glowing like so many red coals in the dim light of the church. Some seemed to be licking their lips, as if in anticipation. "For the meat of the Word," I fervently hoped.

I began. My exordium dealing with the primitive foolishness of literal belief in the devil did not seem to go over very well. Some of the congregation were frowning and others were picking at their hymnals in an irritating fashion.

Then I discussed the temptations as such. The congregation clearly appreciated this much more than the preceding. As I argued that Jesus should have made the stones into bread for others, they smiled—or perhaps "grinned" would better describe it. When I noted parenthetically that Jesus, even as the Ideal Man, could hardly have thwarted the laws of gravitation, they began to show real interest. When I came to the possibility of man's gaining the kingdoms of the world for purposes of social reform, they were positively ecstatic. And they didn't seem to have a bit of trouble with "evolutionary perfection."

This positive reaction should have pleased me, I suppose, but frankly, the effect was just the opposite. As their eyes grew brighter, and as they licked their lips more obviously, I felt the heat rise until I didn't think I could bear it. And—was it possible?—the congregation seemed, if anything to draw closer to the fire, and bundle themselves up to a greater extent in their heavy coats and scarves. In contrast, I found myself trembling with sweat and fear.

Finally something within me snapped. Instead of using the peroration in my notes, I began to preach *ex tempore* on Jesus as Lord and God—being tempted by the devil to renounce His saving purpose for the human race—but conquering the evil one with those magnificent words, "Get thee hence, Satan: for it is written, Thou shalt worship the Lord thy God, and Him only shalt thou serve."

As I sat down, the congregation showed definite signs of irritation. Their eyes no longer glowed very brightly, and some faces looked ashen. No one was licking his lips. The temperature had dropped appreciably.

Oldstone concluded the service—a bit summarily, I thought, but none too soon for me. At the door, he told me that the congregation customarily remained in their pews for Sunday school, but that I needn't stay for that. He emphasized the "needn't." Then he said with an expression of sadness and disappointment: "You were doing wonderfully, my boy, until the last part of the sermon. You ought to change that conclusion; the people didn't like it. I'm sure of that. Too theological for us simple folk. We thought that you'd be able to stay and be, er, a part of our eucharistic service later. From all we heard, you would have fitted beautifully into our little congregation—perhaps on a permanent basis. We haven't had a pastor in many years . . ." He looked wistfully at the communion table, and his pale tongue passed quickly over his thin lips. "But I don't think you're quite ready, my boy. Go back to seminary for a while longer. And THEN COME BACK TO US HERE AT ST. 'POLLYON'S."

These last words were said with almost hypnotic force. I shuddered but did not reply. He turned and proceeded, bug-like, down the nave. I fled to my car and drove like sixty back to Sodom Junction—to Route 6A—to Highway 37—to the seminary. That day I became a theologian.

• • •

"And that's it?" said Cavender with a look combining amazement with authentic concern.

"That's it," I replied. "Except for a little historical background I acquired the following week at the seminary. No one else seemed to know of a St. Paul's church in that locality, so I checked a few old histories of the synod. There had been a church all right, but all the histories agreed that it had burned down in a lightning storm in 1867. One writer said that, in the synod at the time, some suggested maliciously that the fire had been deserved—that the congregation had been cheating on its benevolence budget for years, and that strange goings-on had been reported there from time to time, especially on All Saints' Eve.

"Oh, yes, and one other thing," I added. "When the Dean heard that I had come back from St. Paul's—or St. Apollyon's as they called it—he said to me: 'Glad to see you, young man. I prayed for you much this weekend. It's been some time since one of the men has been called to supply at St. Paul's. I presume that you will want the advanced seminar in dogmatics next year?' 'Praise God,' I answered, 'that is just what I want.'"

"You expect me to roar at the whole thing, don't you?" Cavender asked. "Well, you get a surprise. Sure, I'm a skeptic, but not a fool. That 'more things in heaven and earth' bit is quite sensible. And wasn't it your Luther who said that the devil is God's devil?"

"Quite right, Cavender. And that fits very nicely with the Gospel lesson for that first Sunday in Lent: 'Then was Jesus led up of the Spirit into the wilderness to be tempted of the devil.'"

Epilogue: Before You Close the Creaking Door

*We wrestle not against flesh and blood,
but against principalities, against powers,
against the rulers of the darkness of this
world, against spiritual wickedness in high places.
Wherefore take unto you the whole armor of God.*

—Eph. 6:12–13

A few concluding words are in order both for the evangelical who seeks perspective on the occult and for the general reader whose quest for truth has brought him into contact with "God's devil."

Evangelical believers need a greater measure of maturity when faced with the occult. This judgment may not appear particularly informative, since evangelicals seem to suffer from endemic adolescence (teenage decisions for Christ but few grown-up churches, etc.), but where the occult is involved, evangelical immaturity leads to particularly tragic results. Finding it difficult to handle the occult, the evangelical is alternately fascinated and repelled by occult phenomena. It is a known fact that young people at Christian camps have dabbled quite considerably in the occult in recent years. Converts to church-of-Satan groups very often have a history of fundamentalist upbringing.

What accounts for the fundamentalist fascination with the dark world? At least two considerations. First is the characteristic I dubbed, in an *Eternity* article of some years ago, "kookishness." Kookishness refers to "absurd irrationalism associated with a theological position: nuttiness that produces disrespect for the theology proclaimed in conjunction with it." I illustrated with three areas in which evangelicals have shown themselves to be kooks first-class: prophetically establishing the end of the world in all its details; anti-intellectualism and the setting of "the Spirit" over against serious learning and education; and the embracing of right-wing political and social fanaticisms, such as the conviction (à la *Dr. Strangelove*) that "the international communist conspiracy" is poisoning our free society through fluoridation. Connected with such crackpot ideas are, inevitably, occult notions. When evangelicals become convinced that only they know what is "really" going on (only they see the communist menace in its true gravity, only they are aware of the true naturopathic methods of healing, etc.), a gigantic step has been taken on the road to Mordor's Land. For hiddenness is, as we have been at pains to emphasize, one of the chief aspects of the occult and, indeed, its etymological meaning. The evangelical, in his neurotic defensiveness against a world that so very largely rejects his central convictions, reacts by finding more and more "hidden truths" that the world, in its "spiritual blindness," can only ridicule. Thus the Bible becomes a source of bizarre information on matters that can only puzzle the uninitiated unbeliever—educated though he may be in his own eyes while lacking the true "wisdom." The bridge to the occult is quite clear in the remarks made in an interview on flying saucers by evangelist Frank E. Stranges, author of *Flying Saucerama*, who told his radio audience (KHOF, Los Angeles) on 20th July 1966:

> What we know about U.F.O.s perhaps is summed up in the first chapter of Ezekiel where brother Ezekiel speaks of the wheel within a wheel. In the South African series in my book *Saucerama*, here is one of the finest examples of a wheel in the middle of a wheel. The only

moving part on this craft, in other words, was the outer rotating rim. . . . These are all the same pictures, all the same craft. The only moving part was the outer rim. Now Ezekiel goes on to say the color of the creature—he calls it a creature. It might be interesting to note before we even say that, that he uses the words "eyes were very high and dreadful." That same Hebrew word "eyes" is the same Hebrew word used in Ecclesiastes for "windows." . . . And he says the color of this creature is as the color of beryl, beryllium, the silicate of aluminum. Now the one that crashed off the Helgeland coast some years ago, which is also in the book *Saucerama*, they claim was tougher than steel, and lighter than aluminum!

Here Stranges reveals the true nature of flying saucers, which unbelievers could not fathom, but which an occult reading of Scripture makes crystal clear! The distance to cabalistic Bible interpretation drops virtually to nil. Is it any wonder that evangelicals, forgetting that "the whole armor of God" is all that is needed to stand in an evil world and therefore defensively seeking the occult in the Bible, so readily fall victim to dark influences?

Still another and no less consequential reason why evangelicals are fascinated by the occult is their preoccupation with "spiritual experience." Why do evangelicals prefer revivalistic conversions to conversions of any other type? Why are "testimony meetings" so important in evangelical church life? Why is there such a "cult of personality" surrounding charismatic fundamentalist leaders? Evangelicalism, with its roots in the open-air eighteenth-century English preaching and the nineteenth-century American frontier, centers not on Scripture, church, doctrine, or sacraments, but on personal experience. Having the right kind of conversion, second blessing, "peace," etc. becomes all-important, and without it, all else may be suspect. But since, according to Scripture, experience *itself* must be tested from the outside for divine origin (there being many spirits abroad on the earth), the evangelical who refuses to test the spirits in his own experience courts disaster. To him, the Evil One has only to beckon: "Come to me and I will give you an experience such as you have never had!" The urge for special charismatic gifts and the suspicion toward those without them can become the other side of the coin to a lusting after strange gods. Métraux, in his careful study of voodoo in Haiti, significantly observed: "A Pentecostal preacher describing his feelings when 'the spirit was upon him,' listed to me exactly the same symptoms as those which I had heard from the mouths of people who have been possessed by *loa*."[2] On the positive side, this meant an easy transition from voodoo to Protestantism (so comments Métraux); but negatively it suggests a most perilous experiential focus. If evangelicals were to center their theology and church life on the objective Scriptural verities instead of on the experience which can never be more than a by-product of these verities, they would reach a level of spiritual maturity far more conducive to the proper interpretation of the occult.

But instead of such a balanced approach, the evangelical tendency has been (in this area as in others) to counter one extreme with

---

2. Kurt E. Koch, *Christian Counseling and Occultism*, trans. Andrew Petter (Grand Rapids, Michigan: Kregel, 1965). Cf. also the essay "Schizophrenia and Spiritualism," in Simeon Edmunds's *Spiritualism: A Critical Survey* (London: Aquarian Press, 1966), pp. 187–94.

another. Are our young people fascinated with the occult? Then forbid all contact with it! Here we have an exact parallel with the fundamentalist's general negative reaction to "the world": separate from it. Stay away from the theater, the dance, modern entertainment, secular education, godless books and magazines, etc., etc. Thus treatments of the occult from an evangelical standpoint (even generally responsible treatments) tend to lump all occult phenomena, from scientific ESP experimentation to sorcery, in a single category, which is then labeled "satanic" and the label "Touch Not" affixed to it. The result of such separationism is inevitably to blur the good and the neutral with the bad, and to drive the evangelical who recognizes that not all is bad to reject the entire argument; ironically, therefore, separationism usually produces exactly the evils it tries to counteract! The fundamentalist church in the town in which I grew up, by effectively keeping its young people from all forms of mixed entertainment, succeeded in having the highest illegitimate birth rate of any church in the community!

Moreover, a negative attitude toward all that is occult can blind us to the overwhelmingly important truth (emphasized at various points in this book) that wanderings in the occult labyrinth may be halting attempts to find the way of life. To this possibility, we wish to devote a few closing words.

• • •

If, reader, your interest in the occult has indeed been motivated by a search for the truth, then you and I have taken the right path together. Frankly, I have no interest in doctrinaire occultists, who, like those men of the last times as described by the Apostle, are "ever learning and never able to come to the knowledge of the truth" (2 Tim. 3:7). "Their folly shall be manifest unto all men," says the text, and our study of a diversity of occult philosophies of existence has illustrated that fact without much difficulty.

What is the fundamental failing in the occult perspective? Even before his conversion to Christianity (but on his way toward it), famed Oxford scholar C. S. Lewis recognized the nature of that failing, doubtless in part because he himself had been drawn toward the dark land. Sometime in the 1920s, Lewis corresponded on the subject with Owen Barfield, who would later do irreparable harm to his talent by embracing Rudolf Steiner's occult Anthroposophy. One of Lewis's unpublished and undated letters of that period, written at Magdalen College, is headed "The Real Issue between Us." Lewis first describes his own approach by an analogy based upon Plato's myth of the cave; like every man, Lewis is bound to the post of finite personality so that he cannot turn around and observe reality directly; clouds behind him represent that ultimate reality or True Being. His understanding of the meaning of life comes by observing the mirror before him, which displays "as much of the reality (and such disguise of it) as can be seen" from his position. He devotes himself to studying the mirror with his eyes ("explicit cognition") and also reaches backward with his hands "so as to get some touch (implicit 'taste' or 'faith') of the real." For Barfield the occultist, however, though his position vis-à-vis reality is necessarily the same as Lewis's, his reaction to it is far different. Let Lewis's inimitable pen provide the description:[3]

---

3. Alfred Métraux, *Voodoo in Haiti*, trans. Hugo Charteris (New York: Oxford University Press, 1959), p. 357.

Here we see a gentleman (not identified) engaged on seeing whether a departure from dry academical methods and a newer, freer theory of knowledge may not get some new images out of the mirror. The mirror seems to be playing up well so far. Meanwhile the clouds have ebbed to his ankles. Something like despairing hands stretches to reach from behind but he doesn't notice them. Overhead I detect a curious figuration of cloud that fancy may interpret as a gigantic face in laughter. The hammer and chisel are occult science, yoga, "meditation" (in technical sense) etc.

Text of C. S. Lewis's handwritten caption

Here we see a gentleman (not identified) engaged on seeing whether a departure from dry academical methods and a newer, freer theory of knowledge may not get some new images out of the mirror. The mirror seems to be playing up well so far. Meanwhile the clouds have ebbed to his ankles. Something like despairing hands stretches to reach from behind but he doesn't notice them. Overhead I detect a curious figuration of cloud that fancy may interpret as a gigantic face in laughter. The hammer and chisel are occult science, yoga, "meditation" (in technical sense) etc.

An orful example. Study of a gentleman reaching vainly for the inner reality he has scorned, while he shrinks in horror from the phantom he has created on the black wall from which he has succeeded in chipping off <u>all</u> the looking-glass. (Only those who are not poets cd. get as far as this, of course) On a second mirror invisible to him but visible to his neighbours, ambulance, asylum, cemetery appear successively.

Text of C. S. Lewis's handwritten caption

An orfal example. Study of a gentleman reaching vainly for the inner reality he has scorned, while he shrinks in horror from the phantom he has created on the black wall from which he had succeeding [*sic*; succeeded] in chipping off *all* the looking-glass. (Only those who are not poets could get as far as this, of course) On a second mirror invisible to him but visible to his neighbours, ambulance, asylum, cemetery appears successively.

Barfield's occult efforts to find reality not only do not succeed, but they destroy the only means of discovering reality, they ignore the "despairing hands" reaching out from eternity to save him from folly and the Lord laughing him to derision, and they open the floodgates to the phantoms of another world which are fully capable of driving him successively to "ambulance, asylum, cemetery." Says Lewis earlier in the letter: "All that your occultism can give us is *not* the Real instead of the phenomenal but simply more phenomena less surely grounded (in the empirical way) than the ones we have already, and less real because they claim to be more. For the highest merit of the phenomenon is to *confess* itself a phenomenon." Though Lewis had not yet focused the eyes of explicit cognition on the empirical facticity of Christ's person and work, and thus had the shackles of the human dilemma loosened for him by the Son who alone "makes free indeed" (John 8:36), he saw clearly that there is no shortcut to reality. Occultists think that by shattering ordinary methods of knowing they will reach hidden truth, but their knowledge must come by empirical means also, and it is therefore subject to the same empirical tests as any other truth-claim. This lucid realization kept Lewis on the track in his search for the true meaning of reality, and made it possible for him later to weigh the vapid claims of the occultists against the solid historical evidence that "God was in Christ, reconciling the world unto Himself."

If we are honest with ourselves, we must all admit the profundity of the occult quest. Who is not moved by these words of Arthur Machen, one of the greatest of the supernatural story writers?

> We shall go on seeking it to the end, so long as there are men on the earth. We shall seek it in all manner of strange ways; some of them wise, and some of them unutterably foolish. But the search will never end.
>
> "It?" "It" is the secret of things; the real truth that is everywhere hidden under outward appearances; the end of the story, as it were; the few final words that make every doubtful page in the long book plain, that clear up all bewilderments and all perplexities, and show how there was profound meaning and purpose in passages apparently obscure

and purposeless. These are the words which, once read, throw their light and radiance back over all the book; as the furnace fires blazing up suddenly at night in my own country in the west, shine far away among woods, and in dark valleys, and discover his path to the wanderer in a wild, dim world.

Doubtless there is a secret, an illuminating secret, hidden beneath all the surfaces of things; and perhaps the old alchemists were thinking of that secret when they spoke of the Powder of Projection, the Philosopher's Stone, that turned all it touched into gold.[4]

Yes, there is a secret: the truth behind the appearances; the end of the story. The occult quest is the search for that Stone of the Philosophers capable of turning all to gold. And the Stone is Christ, as the perceptive alchemists discovered. This is the tried and precious Stone laid prophetically in Zion (Isa. 28:16); if any man come in belief to that Christ as to a living Stone,

4. This C. S. Lewis letter is copyrighted by the C. S. Lewis Estate.

he "shall not be confounded" (1 Pet. 2:4–8). Here is the only sure foundation (1 Cor. 3:11). All others are chimerical: the castles of occult experience built upon them will turn to mist when the Sun of righteousness shines upon them. Beware of the magic of Midas, who obtained what appeared to be the golden touch, but it destroyed him. Do not be confounded: in Christ alone "are hid all the treasures of wisdom and knowledge. And this I say, lest any man should beguile you with enticing words" (Col. 2:3–4). The promise stands firm for us as for the men of olden time (Isa. 45:1, 45:17):

> *I will give thee the treasures of darkness,*
> *and hidden riches of secret places,*
> *that thou mayest know that I, the Lord,*
> *which call thee by thy name,*
> *am the God of Israel....*
> *Israel shall be saved in the Lord*
> *with an everlasting salvation:*
> *ye shall not be ashamed nor confounded*
> *world without end.*

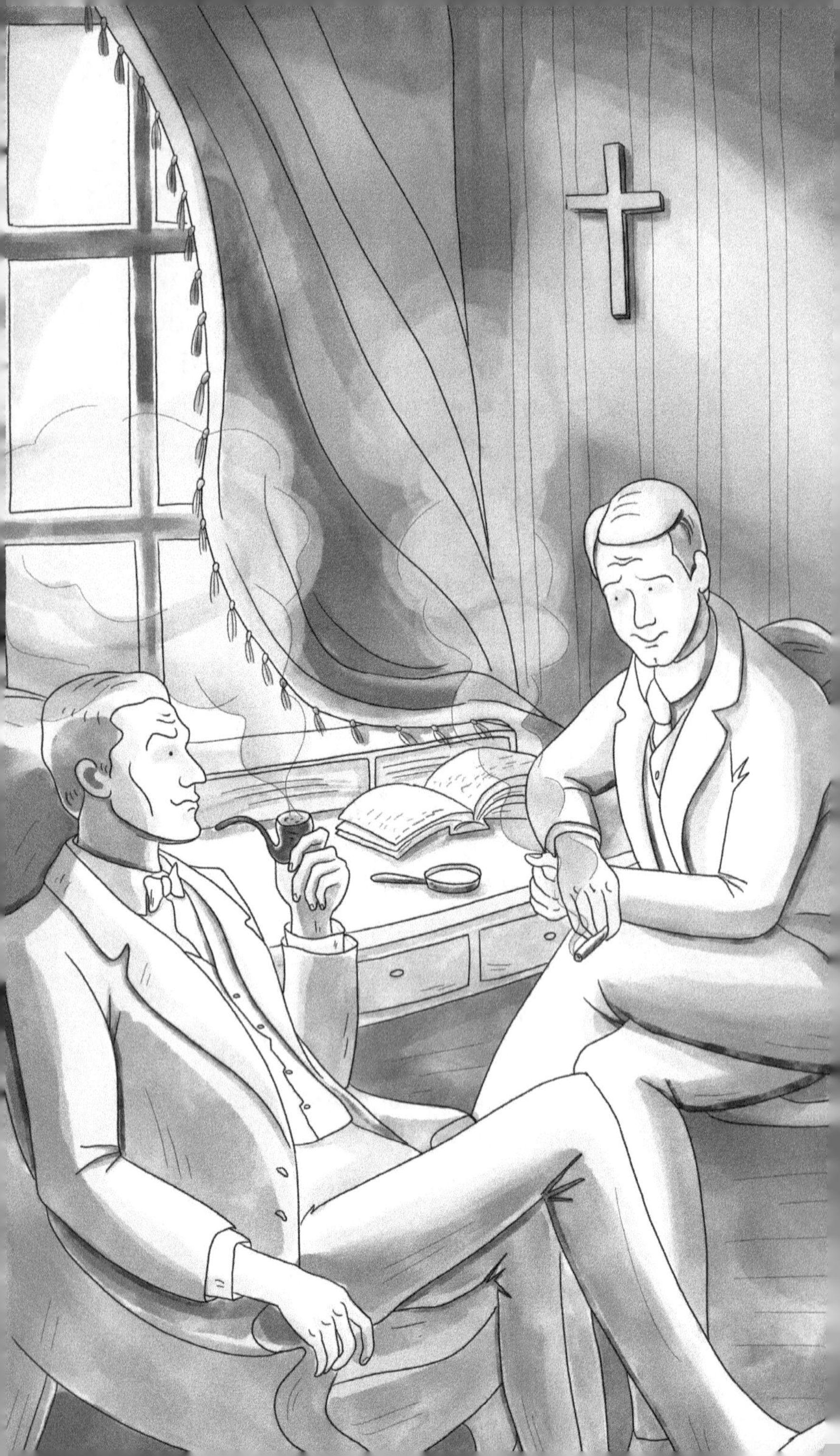

The Search for Ultimates
A SHERLOCKIAN INQUIRY[1]

By way of introduction: the remarkable dialogue to follow came into my hands quite unexpectedly. I had been a member in good standing of The Sherlock Holmes Society of London for a number of years, but it was only on moving permanently to the United Kingdom in 1991 that I was able to participate actively in the Society's affairs. On learning that I was a published theologian as well as an academic, senior members graciously

---

1. An invitational presentation at the twenty-fourth annual philosophy symposium ("Rationality and Spirituality") of the California State University, Fullerton, 11–13 March 1993. Other speakers included D. Z. Phillips and Ninian Smart.

invited me to speak when the subject of discussion touched upon religious concerns. After my response to the Bishop of Durham's address at the Society's forty-first annual dinner on 8th January 1993 at the Langham Hotel, I was taken aside and let in on the Society's most well-guarded secret: that Dr. Watson's battered tin dispatch-box, containing notes of Sherlock Holmes's unpublished cases, had been entrusted to the Society by Lloyds Bank, successor to Cox & Co. (THOR, CREE, VEIL).[2]

Among the yellowing, faded documents in that box was the dialogue which I reproduce here for the first time. It was the Society's wish that it be made known in a responsible theological-philosophical context, in line with the seriousness of the issues addressed. I am humbled at the confidence the Society has placed in me in allowing me to offer the dialogue to a university audience, and I trust that it will encourage those who hear or read it to pursue truth as assiduously as did the Great Detective himself.

---

2. These abbreviations—standard in Sherlockian scholarship—refer to the titles of the stories in the Holmesian canon. (See the abbreviation list at the end of this chapter.)

A Caveat

In order to obviate misunderstanding, I should perhaps emphasize, before presenting the dialogue itself, that no attempt is being made to promote Holmes's (or Watson's) personal religious views as such. Much attention has been devoted to the precise nature of these opinions,[3] and I have myself written on the subject.[4] But, for our present purpose, such questions are irrelevant. The value of the following dialogue lies not in the opportunity it might offer to emulate or criticize a great man's religious views but in the assistance it can provide in arriving at a sound methodology for handling ultimate questions.

Above all, Holmes's strength lay in his methodological rigor: his razor-sharp

---

3. See, for example, the entries under "philosophy" and "religion and morals" in S. Tupper Bigelow, *Bigelow on Holmes: An Index to the Writings*, ed. Donald A. Redmond (Toronto: Metropolitan Toronto Library Board, 1974), pp. 67, 69. Particularly valuable is E. C. D. Stanford's essay "The Beliefs of Sherlock Holmes," *The Sherlock Holmes Journal*, Autumn 1978.
4. John Warwick Montgomery, "Holmes in Tibet," in *The Transcendent Holmes*, rev. ed. (Irvine, California: New Reformation Publications, 2015).

employment of the inferential techniques of deduction, induction, and—especially—what Peirce termed abduction: imaginative, retroductive reasoning, by which constructs were arrived at that succeeded where others had failed in solving apparently intractable factual dilemmas.[5] The genuine seeker after truth should therefore benefit maximally from the methodological guidance Holmes provides, and it is to Holmes's reasoning processes rather than to his own beliefs or lack of them that we direct the listener's and reader's attention in what now follows.

---

5. "Method: A Juxtaposition of Charles S. Peirce and Sherlock Holmes," foreword by Max H. Fisch (Bloomington, Indiana: Gaslight Publications, 1980); and Umberto Eco and Thomas A. Sebeok (eds.), *The Sign of Three: Dupin, Holmes, Peirce* (Bloomington: Indiana University Press, 1988). Cf. also John Warwick Montgomery, "The Theologian's Craft: A Discussion of Theory Formation and Theory Testing in Theology and Science," *American Scientific Affiliation Journal*, September 1966, and frequently reprinted, e.g., in his *The Suicide of Christian Theology* (Newburgh, Indiana: Trinity College Press, 1970), pp. 267–313.

Ultimate Questions: Why Bother?[6]

It was, as I recall, in September 1901, that Holmes and I had the only extended religious conversation in all our years together at 221B Baker Street. Considering Holmes's taciturnity in all matters relating to his personal life (we had known each other for years before I even learned of the existence of his brother Mycroft), it may seem strange that such a conversation ever took place at all. The circumstances were these: September had been a month of trivialities and stagnation,[7] and, as I have noted on more than one occasion, Holmes tolerated inactivity very badly. In his earlier years, before the Reichenbach Falls and the death of Professor Moriarty, periods without a case to stimulate him were often filled with the cocaine needle.

I never wanted to see that again, and so I determined to rouse Holmes from mental

---

6. Section headings have been added by the editor in an effort to underscore the major philosophical and religious issues raised in the dialogue. Where they are unhelpful in clarifying Dr. Watson's text, they should be ignored.
7. Confirmed: Ernest Bloomfield Zeisler, *Baker Street Chronology* (New York: Magico Magazine, 1983), p. 145.

lassitude by drawing him into a subject complex enough that it could not help but stimulate that powerful brain. Philosophical and religious questions, though not of interest to the average, pragmatic Englishman such as myself, enormously fascinated Holmes: had he not commented brilliantly on the Buddhism of Ceylon (SIGN)[8] and visited the head Lama in Tibet during his years of wandering after Reichenbach (EMPT)? So I determined to bait my dear friend for his own good.

"Holmes," I remarked, "do you remember our discussion of the Copernican theory soon after we set up in Mrs. Hudson's cozy digs at 221B? You expressed total indifference to the idea that the earth went around the sun. Your words were, if I recall correctly, 'If we went round the moon it would not make a pennyworth of difference to me or to my work' (STUD). The same is true, is it not, of religious claims?"

From within the dense cloud of pipe smoke that surrounded the head of my

---

8. Identifications of canonical cases have been introduced by the editor to facilitate the cross-referencing of Holmesian materials.

friend, a dissatisfied grunt emerged: my query, like flint, had produced a spark.

"Certainly not, Watson. You confuse two very different things. Practically speaking, our lives are conducted in the same way on this planet whether it is stationary or mobile. But what we do or do not do is profoundly influenced by what we believe the purpose of it all is."

"Really, Holmes," I replied. "How can you say that? The world goes on regardless of the beliefs of its inhabitants."

My friend had now clearly surfaced from his brown study: a game of another sort was afoot.

"You see, Watson, but you do not observe. On the surface, it seems that human life goes on heedless of the beliefs of its principals. But consider: if a man—like the late, unlamented Professor Moriarty—does not believe in a final judgment, he will endeavor to achieve his ends by whatever mischief he thinks will go undetected. And since the efficacy of the forces of order is distinctly finite (I think of friend Lestrade) such a man—or woman—becomes, potentially if not actually, a source of immense and uncontrollable evil."

"But surely, Holmes, the average person is no Moriarty."

"Quite right, Watson. But this is because the man on the Clapham omnibus lives from inherited capital. In our age of increasing secularization, he assumes—without thinking much, if at all, about it—that there are moral absolutes and a final reckoning. If he lives consistently with any other view, he would pose the dangers of Moriarty, Colonel Sebastian Moran, and their ilk. Thus the issue of religious truth is of the most capital importance."

The Need for a Transcendent Ethic

As Holmes warmed to the bait, I determined to strike deeper. How often has my dear friend underestimated my reasoning abilities—admittedly far less than his own but (if I may say so) capable of pursuing a worthy quarry!

"Holmes," I cried, "you do not do yourself justice. A last judgment is not needed to sustain morality. All that is needed is a consensus of right-thinking folk, such as we have here in this blessed green land of England."

"Consensus, Watson?" Holmes snapped. "Even if such a consensus is granted—and

I predict that as the movements of peoples increase in this new century even England will soon be unable to boast of one—what is the justification of that consensus? Fifty million Frenchmen can be wrong: you would surely admit *that*. But it follows inexorably that the same may be true of fifty million Englishmen. Water does not rise above its own level. A society's morality cannot rise above the level of those who create it. What assurance do we have that a given consensus represents true goodness? Without such assurance, the *vox populi* can as well represent, not the *vox dei* but the *vox diaboli*. No, Watson, a moral consensus is not enough. A true ethic will need to be a transcendental ethic. Was it not Rousseau who declared, 'It would take gods to give men laws'?"[9]

The Diversity of Religious Claims

"I take your point. Holmes," I conceded, "but it gets us nowhere. Even if one admits that a relativistic, acculturated morality is

9. Holmes refers to the *Contract Social*, Bk. 2, chap. 7. Cf. John Warwick Montgomery, "The Case for 'Higher Law,'" *Law & Justice*, No. 112/113 (Hilary/Easter 1992), pp. 31–50.

an insufficient basis for human interaction, that hardly justifies leaping into the arms of religion. Are you suggesting, as some philosophers do, that we can solve the problem by accepting some kind of generalized transcendent belief—that all religions really say the same thing and bring us to the same ultimate goal?"[10]

"I am surprised at you, Watson. After what we learned of Mormon treachery and the bizarre nature of that cult's belief-system (STUD), do you seriously think that I could maintain the functional or theoretical equivalency of all religious viewpoints? I can only agree with what I read somewhere"—here Holmes's bony arm shot forth to grasp one of his commonplace books and his nervous fingers quickly found the page containing the clipping he sought. "Ah, here it is:

---

10. This view persists in our own time among some religious thinkers. Thus Ninian Smart, in his 1979–80 Gifford Lectures, advocates "the complementarity of Buddhism and Christianity. They are different ways of going towards the Beyond" ("Postscript: Towards a New Worldview: The Pacific Mind," *Beyond Ideology: Religion and the Future of Western Civilization* [London: Collins, 1981], p. 309).

For the Christian it is not necessary to abstain from alcohol; for the Muslim it is. For the one, a pilgrimage to Mecca is not even encouraged; for the other it is, given the means, *de rigueur*. For one pacifism may have to be taken much more seriously than for the other. For one, one wife; for the other, maybe more.

For one Christ is God; for the other this claim is blasphemous. What good is then achieved by saying that the two worship the same God? . . . There are restrictions of two sorts upon the fruitfulness of making identifications. One is that full identification is not possible because of contradictions in the respective full ramified concepts (of God and of Allah, say); the other is that at the lower end—reaching a degree of abstraction in the description of the identified being leads to vacuity.[11]

11. Remarkably, this quotation closely parallels a passage in a work written many years later: Ninian Smart, *The Concept of Worship* (London: Macmillan, 1972), pp. 72–73. Even more remarkably, the author's argument here did not seem significantly to impact the viewpoint he presented seven years later (see our immediately preceding note). True, Smart speaks of "religious" or "'theological' rather than

"And this is only the tip of the iceberg. If all the great religious and metaphysical claims were merely contradictory, choosing one in preference to another would be a harmless activity—rather like choosing to collect stamps as a hobby instead of going into coin-collecting. No one would be any the wiser as to the actual nature of things or as to ultimate values, but little harm would be done.

"However, Watson," and here a dark shadow crossed my friend's brow, "we must never forget that ultimate claims are *not* neutral. Far from it. How many horrors have been committed in the name of false religions! To take but a single example: the Aztecs engaged, you will remember, in human sacrifice. This was not peripheral to their belief-system: it was the very center of it. Religious commitment can lead to the most terrifying results. Indeed, if we include political faiths within the ambit of our discussion, one can

---

'phenomenological'" grounds for legitimating the identification of two or more contradictory beliefs as constituting worship of the same God, but this gratuitous dualism merely begs the question: why should a higher, "theological" level of validity exist in the face of clear phenomenological contradiction?

well imagine the terrors that such fanaticism could produce. Perhaps the anarchists of our day are but a precursor of horrendous and destructive mass movements of the future. No, Watson, it is a false and deceptive analogy that sees the world's religions as no more than diverse paths leading up a mountain to the same summit."

Holmes's reference to anarchists and the growth of political religions at some vague future date appeared to me utterly fanciful, and I said as much. I reminded Holmes that though we had just lost our dear Queen,[12] her enlightened policies were continuing under the aegis of her son and that the greatest Empire the world had ever seen would go forward in its task of enlightening the globe. I did not appreciate the look of pained irony on my friend's face as he listened to my rebuke, but I determined not to allow the discussion to stray from its original course. Politics would not hold Holmes's interest for long; ultimate questions might well do so.

---

12. Queen Victoria passed away on Tuesday, 22nd January 1901, and was succeeded by her son Edward, Prince of Wales (as Edward VII).

Consistency and Elegance as Truth-Tests

"Suppose we grant for the sake of argument your general point that all religions might be false but certainly cannot all be true," I continued. "The need to find a transcendent basis for morality will then require us to arbitrate the diversity of religious claims. We shall have to separate the wheat (if any) from the chaff. What criteria could we possibly employ in such a high endeavor?"

"Ah, Watson, there you surpass yourself: you have touched the nerve of the problem—the issue of proof. Let us see how well you have learned my methods. I shall describe the most widely accepted answer to your question as maintained by the philosophers and religionists of our day, and you will tell me if they are right.

"Hegel and our own F. H. Bradley[13] speak for the philosophical community and especially for the religious philosophers as they set forth their grandiose metaphysical conceptions. They expect us to accept their

---

13. Holmes doubtless has in mind Bradley's great work, *Appearance and Reality*, first published in 1893.

theories on the twin grounds of internal consistency and aesthetic elegance. Ought we so to do?"

Whilst Holmes went to the mantelpiece and transferred some more of his foul-smelling shag from the Persian slipper to his pipe, I ruminated on his question. I determined to gain time by answering with a question of my own.

"But surely, Holmes, these idealistic metaphysicians do not so restrict themselves; they must maintain that their views fit reality better than the views of others?"

"True, they do sometimes use such language, Watson, and you are to be commended for raising the point. But you will observe that they deny any independent factual test of truth, for they hold that one's metaphysic decides one's epistemology—one's method of evaluating fact. It follows inexorably that for them the choice of belief-system determines what is or is not factual truth and cannot therefore be examined by independent factual testing. So I return to my original question: do we accept their views on the basis of their internal consistency and metaphysical elegance?"

"You push me to my very limits, Holmes. I am but a humble doctor, not a philosopher. But I recall, in my medical practice, numerous cases of madmen whose views of the world have been entirely consistent, even aesthetically elegant, and yet utterly wrong-headed. Recall the sad case of Colonel Warburton (ENGR). No, Holmes, I believe that I must reject the contention of the renowned philosophers of religion to whom you refer."

"Good old Watson! As I shall doubtless say more than once, since it bears repeating: 'You are the one fixed point in a changing age' (last). Your analysis is perfectly correct. The man who is convinced that he is followed everywhere by Albanians may be entirely consistent and his story may have a high degree of aesthetic interest, but he is no less grist for the alienist's mill for all that."

The Issue of Factuality

"If we wish to arbitrate metaphysical and religious claims," Holmes went on, "the *sine qua non* is to appreciate the unyielding nature of the factual world about us. We do not create it by our philosophical speculations or religious ecstasies: it meets us at every turn, insisting that our ultimate claims conform to it. How many times in our myriad investigations have I cried, 'Data, data, data' (STUD, COPP, SHOS, SCAN)? Is it not self-evident that 'I can discover facts, but I cannot change them' (THOR)? Indeed, my very career and the successes, modest though they be, that I have achieved rest squarely upon the principle that it is always *a capital mistake to theorize in advance of the facts* (SECO).

"Religion is one with ordinary life—with science, with law, with detection, with the decision-making we engage in every day of our lives. First, the intractable data must be established, the facts determined: then, and only then, will one be in a position to theorize with any hope of reaching a satisfactory solution. Any other route leads inexorably to the mountains of madness."

"But Holmes," I cried, "factual data never led us to certainty, and certainty is precisely what religion is all about."

"You never cease to amaze me, Watson. I would never have taken you to be a reader of Lessing. His writings are a far cry from Clark Russell's fine sea stories in which you not infrequently indulge (FIVE)."

"Do not patronize me, Holmes. You know that I have never read Lessing."

"No insult intended, Watson. I was merely pointing out that, as usual, you are more perceptive than you yourself realize. The German Enlightenment philosopher Lessing maintained that an impassable gulf—a ditch—separates factual reality from religious truth, for the former necessarily consists of probabilities, whilst the latter demands absolute certainty.

"But Lessing and his ilk make a grave epistemological error. They confuse mathematical certainty with religious certainty. In mathematics, or in deductive logic, one arrives at absolute certainty simply because one reasons from the accepted premises of the system. But there is no necessary connection with the real world; non-Euclidean geometries are as 'certain' as Euclid's proofs.

"Religion, however, is surely not a matter of pure formality. It deals with the most central factual matters of human existence: man's nature, his destiny, whether and how he can be saved or otherwise made right with the universe. Such factual questions require factual data to resolve them, and where facts are concerned, one never rises to the level of absolute certainty. One must be satisfied with probability."

"You fall into Lessing's very ditch by such an admission. Holmes," I replied. "How can one expect a one hundred percent religious commitment when the case for it can never reach one hundred percent evidentially?"

"Think, Watson! When we cross the Strand from the north side to the south so as to enter Simpson's for a delectable repast, do we have one hundred percent certainty of not being run down by a demented or reckless cabbie?"

"Indeed not."

"And do we take a mere percentage of ourselves across the Strand—corresponding to the evidential likelihood of avoiding traffic?"

"Of course not. We take all of ourselves across."

"Well, then. You see but you do not observe. Every day of our lives, we commit our total selves on the basis of less than one hundred percent evidence. This is part and parcel of life. Religious commitment asks no more—and no less—of us than does ordinary experience."

"I see your point, Holmes. In my medical practice, it is the same. I prescribe *materia medica* on the basis of probabilities—the probability that the given remedy is in fact a specific for the patient's illness as I have diagnosed it to the best of my abilities. But when the patient takes the prescribed dose, he commits himself one hundred percent—his life may well depend upon it."

"Precisely, Watson. The same can be illustrated in every sphere of life. The jury returns its verdict based upon a preponderance of evidence in a civil case or upon 'moral certainty, beyond reasonable doubt' in a criminal case. In neither instance is the verdict a matter of absolute, mathematical certainty. Yet a man's entire estate—indeed, his head—may be severed as a consequence of that verdict."[14]

---

14. Cf. John Warwick Montgomery, *Human Rights and Human Dignity* (2nd ed.; Edmonton, Alberta: Canadian Institute for Law, Theology and Public Policy, 1995), chap. 6. Today, the civil jury has virtually been abolished in England; in Holmes's day, it still functioned (as it does—by constitutional warrant—in the United States).

How Much Evidence for Religious Commitment?

My legs were becoming as stiff as my brain. Quite frankly, I was not used to such discussions. I rose from my chair and went to the bow window of our sitting-room and looked out onto an almost deserted Baker Street. It was close to midnight and patches of yellow fog chased each other, while high above, the full moon played hide-and-seek with strange cloud formations. I thought of my elder brother, who had died of drink not long before the Sholto case (SIGN). How important it was to make the right decisions in life! I resolved to push our discussion to the limit, considering the importance of the issues at stake.

"Your reasoning certainly is plausible. Holmes," I resumed. "But it leaves unanswered the one vital question: what kind of evidence could provide a sufficient reason for accepting one ultimate religious claim over against the others?"

"Ah, Watson, I never get your limits. There are indeed unexplored possibilities about you, as I have noted on more than one occasion (SUSS). You have put your finger on the pulse of the matter. The key to religious verification must surely lie in any claim to God's having revealed himself to us poor mortals. For such a claim to be sustained, it would have to be supported by evidence of acts attributable to God and not to mere man."

"Surely, Holmes, you are not referring to miracles? Even I, with the limited philosophical baggage I carry, recall David Hume's decimation of miracle-arguments for religious truth!"

"Patience, my friend, patience. We shall follow the spoor of miracles very shortly. But first consider revelational evidence from fulfilled prophecy: Have you perused the remarkable volume entitled. *The Coming Prince*, by our old friend Sir Robert Anderson?"[15]

---

15. Sir Robert Anderson, *The Coming Prince* (reprint ed.; Grand Rapids, Michigan: Kregel, n.d.). For the relevant passage, see John Warwick Montgomery (ed.), *Jurisprudence: A Book of Readings* (4th corrected ed.; Strasbourg, France: International Scholarly Publishers, 1992), pp. 494–97; and addendum below. Sir Robert was an admirer of Holmes, in spite of the latter's proclivity to criticize professional law enforcers and occasional cavalier attitude toward legal niceties (see our essay, "Holmes, the Law, and the Inns of

"Not the Assistant Commissioner of Metropolitan Police at the time of the Ripper murders?"[16]

"The very same. Sir Robert may not have found the deranged killer (and I can hardly fault him, for it was also one of my thankfully few unsuccessful cases), but he is a masterful, if amateur, biblical scholar. The book to which I refer shows, conclusively in my view, that the Daniel prophecies of the Messiah-to-come were chronologically

---

Court," in *Transcendent Holmes*). In a popular article, "Sherlock Holmes, Detective, as Seen by Scotland Yard" (*T.P.'s Weekly*, II/47 [2 October 1903], 557–58), Anderson wrote that Watson's "purpose has been not to give us pattern cases of crime detection in order to instruct police officers in their duties ... but to promote in all of us the habit of thinking; and to teach us, as he himself expresses it, 'to think analytically'—'to think backward.' All classes of the community may profit by this lesson; and by none is it more needed than by those who fancy they need it least, our scientific experts and teachers of science." (My appreciation to Richard Lancelyn Green, who introduced me to *T.P.'s Weekly* and the Anderson article.) On Anderson, see especially Dr. A. P. Moore-Anderson, *Sir Robert Anderson: A Tribute and Memoir* (London: Morgan, 1919).

16. See Paul Begg et al., *The Jack the Ripper A to Z* (London: Headline, 1991), pp. 11–18; and cf. Donald Rumbelow, *Jack the Ripper: The Complete Casebook* (reprint ed.; Chicago: Contemporary Books, 1988).

fulfilled to an exactitude in the birth and life of Jesus of Nazareth. Consider, Watson: if the Bible does contain such accurate predictions—and the Daniel prophecy is but one of many highly specific predictions set forth by a diversity of Old Testament writers across the centuries preceding the coming of our Lord—what can account for this? It is not given to us humble and limited creatures to see into the fog-bound future. Such fulfilled predictions call out for a transcendent explanation and serve in principle to validate the revelatory character of the Book containing them."[17]

"I confess that I cannot offer any other reasonable explanation," I replied. "But it is the miracle question that especially piques my curiosity. Am I to assume that you reject Hume's classic argument? 'What choice is left to me, old fellow?' The argument is perfectly circular."

"I do not follow you, Holmes."

"Listen, Watson, Hume contends[18] that 'uniform experience' precludes the miraculous.

---

17. Cf. John Warwick Montgomery (ed.), *Evidence for Faith* (Richardson, Texas: Probe, 1991), passim.
18. *Enquiry Concerning Human Understanding*, sec. X ("Of Miracles"). See John Warwick Montgomery, *The*

Thus if someone—Lestrade, for example—were to tell us that he saw a hansom cab fly, we would always prefer the explanation that he was mistaken or lying to the actuality of the miraculous event."

"And so?"

"There are times, Watson, when your density is indeed breathtaking. How does Hume's conviction of so-called 'uniform experience' come about in the first place? Quite clearly by *observation*: observation of the world in which we all find ourselves. But he cannot then use the abstraction of supposed uniformity to rule out particular evidences of nonuniform behavior! He must give serious attention to claims of nonuniformity and, should the facts so warrant, modify his generalization to take those facts into account. The trouble with philosophers, Watson, is that they continually try to find ways of circumventing the investigation of factual particulars.[19] But it is in the particulars that

---

Shape of the Past (2nd rev. ed.; Minneapolis: Bethany, 1975), especially pp. 289–93, 296–98.
19. Holmes's critique at this point applies equally to Hume's successors, such as Antony Flew. See John Warwick Montgomery, *Faith Founded on Fact* (Nashville: Thomas Nelson, 1978), pp. 43–73.

all knowledge is to be found. Have I not told you more than once: 'Never trust to general impressions' (IDEN)?"

"Your reasoning certainly is plausible," I responded, "but even if Hume does fall into the abyss of *petitio principii*, it does not automatically follow that miracles can vindicate revelation-claims. I recently read somewhere: 'Miracles by themselves could not serve as conclusive evidence of a divine revelation. . . . One needs a prior acceptance and understanding of the idea of God. . . . A miracle is not an external guarantee of the truth of revelation.'"[20]

"Do you take me for a dunderhead, Watson? Of course Hume's illogic does not establish that a given miracle would conclusively guarantee an alleged revelation as divine. But I must take serious issue with your unnamed source when he says that one would first have to know God before a miracle could be regarded as divinely revelatory.

"If a miracle were genuinely performed, we would in theory have two and only two

---

20. Watson's source here cannot be identified. But this passage later appears almost verbatim in Ninian Smart, *Philosophers and Religious Truth* (London: SCM Press, 1964), p. 56.

sources for explaining it: we could ask the miracle-worker for his explanation, or we could seek elsewhere for an explanation—among those who did not and cannot perform it (such as religious philosophers, for example). The rational choice is to seek an explanation from the one who did it, not from those who do not know how to do it themselves. And if the miracle-worker explains the miracle by claiming to be God, Who are we to deny it? *Voilà*: our knowledge of God will grow out of the miracle itself and out of the miracle-worker's presentation of, and teaching about, himself."

"Wait a moment, Holmes," I cried. "You surely are not suggesting that the mere performance of any miracle—any unique event incapable of mere human fabrication—would warrant attributing deity to the perpetrator as long as he claimed to be divine."

"Not at all, Watson. Everything depends on the nature of the miraculous act. Only if it touches the center of our human condition would it require such attribution. An example may help. Suppose Mrs. Hudson were miraculously to produce talking kippers and claim, on that basis, to be divine. Would we worship her?"

"Obviously not, Holmes. In the first place, revelational language demands that God not be female—in spite of the activities of Mrs. Pankhurst and other well-meaning, but misguided, advocates of femininity."

"Really, Watson. We have not yet definitively established the revelatory character of the Scriptures. That depends, both on the prophetic evidence already adduced, and on a showing that our Lord, having demonstrated his deity by rising again from the dead, placed a divine stamp of approval on the sacred text.[21] Do not put the cart before the horse. But I would have to agree with you that once we do arrive at demonstrable revelation, we can hardly play fast and loose with the picture of God it presents to us, even if that picture offends our sensibilities or those of our contemporaries. Shall we, however, return to the point?"

"Forgive me. Holmes," I replied, chagrined. "My second reason for rejecting Mrs. Hudson's claim to deity is that, despite the truly admirable nature of her kippers

---

21. Cf. John Warwick Montgomery (ed.), *God's Inerrant Word: An International Symposium on the Trustworthiness of Scripture* (Minneapolis: Bethany, 1974), passim.

(were the hour not so late, I should ring for a plate of them at this very moment), they do not touch the well-springs of human need."

"Precisely, old fellow. But now take a very different case. Suppose one were to rise again from the dead, raise others also, and promise to give everlasting life to everyone who trusted him. What, then?"

I fell into silence. The memory of my dear young wife Mary, who had passed away so suddenly during the years after Reichenbach when I also thought Holmes dead, overwhelmed me. Tears welled up in my eyes. I would literally give anything in this world or in the next to see her again. "I would worship him as a God if that were indeed true," I replied brokenly.

"Of course you would, Watson," Holmes said softly as he reached over to me and patted my arm. "No one would ever find a greater reason to worship. Have I not said in another connection, 'If there is not some compensation hereafter, then the world is a cruel jest' (VEIL)? Should we be given proof that there is indeed a hereafter and a way to experience blessedness there, we would be fully justified in accepting joyously the divine claim connected therewith.

"Moreover, Watson, you will recall that our Lord's triumph over death was also presented by Him as evidence that He had died a sacrificial death to free us from our damnable selfishness. This squarely fits our knowledge of the human condition and offers us an escape from its consequences.[22] What could be more fundamental or more a legitimation of the divine claims of the One who rose again? I stand by what I have said before: 'The example of patient suffering is in itself the most precious of all lessons to an impatient world' (VEIL)."

"But what colossal claims, Holmes!" I retorted. "What evidence could ever bring one to conviction that Jesus did in fact conquer death? God knows, I want to believe it with all my heart, but how can I?"

"Watson, Watson. How easily the emotions cloud the brain. Think on it: a resurrection

---

22. Holmes's contact with the criminal mind left him with no illusions as to man's fallen state. Quoting Romans 6:23, he declares, "The wages of sin, Watson—the wages of sin! . . . Sooner or later it will always come" (ILLU). And in COPP, there is the well-known passage: "It is my belief, Watson, founded upon my experience, that the lowest and vilest alleys in London do not present a more dreadful record of sin than does the smiling and beautiful countryside."

signifies death at point A and life again at point B. We know what it means to be alive; we also know what death entails. True, we meet life and death in reverse order where resurrection is concerned, but that is irrelevant to the issue of proof. All we need is good eyewitness evidence that Jesus was truly dead and later truly alive. The accounts provide exactly that.[23] Eyewitnesses inform us that he ate fish after Easter morning; none of the corpses we have encountered in our many adventures have managed that."

"But how do we know that the witnesses were reliable, Holmes?"

"Do you remember the curious incident of the dog in the night-time, Watson?"

"To be sure. Our good inspector observed that the dog had done nothing in the night-time, and you responded, 'That was the curious incident' (SILV)."

"Correct, Watson. I wished to impress upon our esteemed colleague that it can be of capital importance if the subject does not

---

23. On the matter of the Gospel records as eyewitness, non-hearsay evidence, see John Warwick Montgomery, *Where Is History Going? Essays in Support of the Historical Truth of the Christian Revelation* (reprint ed.; Minneapolis: Bethany, 1972).

react as all logic dictates that he should. The dog had every reason to bark and he did not do so! Do you suppose that the religious leaders of Jesus' day, having participated in His crucifixion to get rid of Him, would have sat idly by and said and written nothing to counter the Gospel accounts of His miraculous ministry and resurrection had they been in a position factually to refute it?"

"Surely not. Why, they would have been the first to show it all up as a fraud. As the lawyers say, they had means, motive, and opportunity."

"Bravo, Watson. The silence of the hostile witnesses is like that dog in the night-time. It tells us far more than any words could reveal. They kept silence—they did not refute the Gospel witnesses—for one reason and one reason only: they had nothing to say.

"The great miracle of the Resurrection may be a hard metaphysical pill to swallow, but swallow we can and must when the facts require it. Eliminate the factually impossible, and 'whatever remains, however improbable, *must be the truth*' (SIGN)."

The pale light of a London dawn had for some time been stealing into our sitting room. The sound of activity in the kitchen below reminded me that Mrs. Hudson (of the kippers) had already begun her daily tasks. My friend stretched his long legs, placed his tapered, musician's hands behind his neck, and fixed me with his penetrating, deep-set, gray eyes.

"Watson," said he. "As I have told you again and again, I am a brain; all else is mere appendage. But what we have discussed this night requires far more than mere intellectual acquiescence. I read somewhere, and it is profoundly true: 'There is no theoretical knowledge of God. . . . The man who construes religious belief as a theoretical affair distorts it.'[24] As I said to poor, disfigured Eugenia Render—and, thank God, she listened to me, 'Your life is not your own' (VEIL).

"If the case for God's revelation of Himself in His Son our Lord is as powerful as we have found it to be, we shall have to commit ourselves to Him with head and heart, even as, old fellow, you have committed yourself so often to our friendship, and as we both committed ourselves to the service of a certain

---

24. The same argument is presented by D. Z. Phillips in his essay "Faith, Scepticism and Religious Understanding," included in Phillips's *Religion and Understanding* (Oxford: Blackwell, 1967), p. 79.

gracious Lady.[25] And the commitment I now refer to should mean, old friend, that when our detecting days are over we shall meet once again—on a Baker Street that never suffers redevelopment and in company with all those whom we have so inadequately but sincerely loved."

John H. Watson, MD.

Addendum

"The Coming Prince"[26]

The following is from Chapter 10 of *The Coming Prince*, by Sir Robert Anderson, and is quoted for the purpose of illustrating an exactly fulfilled prophecy and the care with which this Christian lawyer examined the Bible.

---

25. Holmes here refers to Queen Victoria. His appeal for commitment grounded in rationality has received modern support in Ronald de Sousa's *The Rationality of Emotion* (Cambridge, Massachusetts: MIT Press, 1987).
26. Reproduced from Irwin H. Linton, Esq., *A Lawyer Examines the Bible* (Boston: W. A. Wilde, 1943), pp. 220–23.

"The secret things belong unto the Lord our God; but those things which are revealed belong unto us and to our children" (Deut. 29:29). And among the "things which are revealed," fulfilled prophecy has a foremost place. In the presence of the events in which it has been accomplished, its meaning lies upon the surface. . . . The writings of Daniel have been more the object of hostile criticism than any other portion of the Scripture, and the closing verses of the ninth chapter have always been a principal point of attack. And necessarily so, for if that single passage can be proved to be a prophecy it establishes the character of a book as a Divine revelation.

The words of Daniel with which Sir Robert Anderson here deals are the following:

Seventy weeks are determined upon thy people and upon thy holy city, to finish the transgression and to make an end of sins and to make reconciliation for iniquity, and to bring in everlasting righteousness, and to seal up the vision and prophecy and anoint the most Holy.

> Know therefore and understand that from the going forth of the commandment to restore and build Jerusalem unto the Messiah the Prince shall be seven weeks and threescore and two weeks: the street shall be built again and the wall even in troublous times.
>
> And after three score and two weeks shall Messiah be cut off, but not for himself . . . (Dan. 9:24–26)

Resuming the quotation from *The Coming Prince*:

> The sceptre of earthly power which was entrusted to the house of David was transferred to the Gentiles in the person of Nebuchadnezzar, to remain in Gentile hands "until the times of the Gentiles be fulfilled."
>
> The blessings promised to Judah and Jerusalem were postponed till after a period described as "seventy weeks"; and at the close of the sixty-ninth week of this era the Messiah should be "cut off."
>
> These seventy weeks represent seventy times seven prophetic years of 360 days, to be reckoned from the

issuing of the edict for the rebuilding of the city—"the street and rampart" of Jerusalem.

The edict in question was the decree issued by Artaxerxes Longimanus in the twentieth year of his reign, authorizing Nehemiah to rebuild the fortifications of Jerusalem.

The date of Artaxerxes' reign can be definitely ascertained—not from elaborate disquisitions by Biblical commentators and prophetic writers, but by the united voice of secular historians and chronologers.

The statement of St. Luke is explicit and unequivocal, that our Lord's public ministry began in the fifteenth year of Tiberius Caesar. It is equally clear that it began shortly before the Passover. The date of it can thus be fixed as between August AD 28 and April AD 29. The Passover of the crucifixion therefore was in AD 32, when Christ was betrayed on the night of the Paschal Supper, and put to death on the day of the Paschal Feast.

If then the foregoing conclusions be well founded we should expect to find that the period intervening between the edict of Artaxerxes and the Passion was 483 prophetic years. And accuracy as absolute as the nature of the case permits is no more than men here are entitled to demand. There can be no loose reckoning in a Divine chronology; and if God has deigned to mark on human calendars the fulfilment of His purposes as foretold in prophecy, the strictest scrutiny shall fail to detect miscalculation or mistake.

The Persian edict which restored the autonomy of Judah was issued in the Jewish month Nisan. It may in fact have been dated the 1st Nisan, but no other date being named, the prophetic period must be reckoned, according to a practice common with the Jews, from the Jewish New Year's Day.[27] The seventy weeks are therefore to be computed from the 1st Nisan BC 445.

Now the great characteristic of the Jewish sacred year has remained unchanged ever since the memorable

---

27. "On the 1st of Nisan is a new year for the computation of the reign of kings and for festivals"—Mishna, treatise "Rosh Hash."

night when the equinoctial moon beamed down upon the huts of Israel in Egypt, bloodstained by the Paschal sacrifice; and there is neither doubt nor difficulty in fixing within narrow limits the Julian date of the 1st of Nisan in any year whatever. In BC 445 the new moon by which the Passover was regulated was on the 13th of March at 7h. 9m. a.m.[28] And

---

28. For this calculation, I am indebted to the courtesy of the Astronomer Royal, whose reply to my inquiry on the subject is appended:

Royal Observatory, Greenwich

June 26th, 1877

Sir:—

I have had the moon's place calculated from Largeteau's Tables in Additions to the Connaissance des Temps 1846, by one of my assistants, and have no doubt of its correctness. The place being calculated for 444, March 12d. 20h, French reckoning, or March 12d. 8h. P.M., it appears that the said time was short of New Moon by about 8h. 47m., and therefore the New Moon occurred at 4h. 47m. A.M., March 13th, Paris time.

I am, etc.,

(Signed) G. B. Airy

accordingly the 1st Nisan may be assigned to the 14th March.

But the language of the prophecy is clear: "From the going forth of the commandment to restore and build Jerusalem unto Messiah the Prince shall be seven weeks and threescore and two weeks." An era therefore of sixty-nine "weeks" or 483 prophetic years reckoned from 14th March BC 445 should close with some event to satisfy the words "unto Messiah the Prince." ...

No student of the gospel narrative can fail to see that the Lord's last visit to Jerusalem was not only in fact, but in the purpose of it, the crisis of His ministry, the goal toward which it had been directed. After the first tokens had been given that the nation would reject His Messianic claims. He had shunned all public recognition of them. But now the twofold testimony of His words and His works had been fully rendered, and His entry into the Holy City was to

---

The new moon, therefore, occurred at Jerusalem on the 13th March, BC 445 (444 Astronomical) at 7h. 9m. A.M.

proclaim His Messiahship and to receive His doom. Again and again His apostles even had been charged that they should not make Him known. But now He accepted the acclamations of "the whole multitude of the disciples," and silenced the remonstrance of the Pharisees with the indignant rebuke, "I tell you if these should hold their peace the stones would immediately cry out." . . .

The time of Jerusalem's visitation had come, and she knew it not. Long ere then the nation had rejected Him, but this was the predestined day when their choice must be irrevocable;—the day so distinctly signalized in Scripture as the fulfilment of Zechariah's prophecy, "Rejoice greatly, O daughter of Zion! shout, O daughter of Jerusalem! behold thy King cometh unto thee." Of all the days of the ministry of Christ upon earth, no other will satisfy so well the angel's words "unto Messiah the Prince."

And the date of it can be ascertained. In accordance with the Jewish custom, the Lord went up to Jerusalem on the 8th

Nisan, "six days before the Passover."[29] But as the 14th, on which the Paschal Supper was eaten, fell that year upon a Thursday, the 8th was the preceding Friday. He must have spent the Sabbath, therefore, at Bethany;[30] and on the evening of the 9th, after the Sabbath had ended, the Supper took place in Martha's house. Upon the following day, the 10th Nisan, He entered Jerusalem as recorded in the Gospels (Lewin, *Fasti Sacri*, p. 230).

The Julian date of that 10th Nisan was Sunday the 6th April, AD 32. What then was the length of the period intervening between the issuing of the decree to rebuild Jerusalem and the public advent of "Messiah the Prince"—between the 14th March BC 445, and the 6th April, AD 32? THE INTERVAL CONTAINED EXACTLY AND TO THE VERY DAY 173,880 DAYS, OR SEVEN TIMES

---

29. "When the people were come in great crowds to the feast of unleavened bread on the eighth day of the month Xanthicus," i.e., *Nisan* (Josephus, *Wars*, vi: 5, 3).
30. "And the Jews' Passover was nigh at hand: and many went out of the country up to Jerusalem, before the Passover, to purify themselves. . . . Then Jesus six days before the Passover, came to Bethany" (John 11:55, 12:1).

SIXTY-NINE PROPHETIC YEARS OF 360 DAYS, the first sixty-nine weeks of Gabriel's prophecy.[31]

31. The 1st Nisan in the twentieth year of Artaxerxes (the edict to rebuild Jerusalem) was 14th March BC 445.

The 10th Nisan in Passion Week (Christ's entry into Jerusalem) was 6th April, AD 32.

The intervening period was 476 years and 24 days (the days being reckoned inclusively, as required by the prophecy, and in accordance with Jewish practice).

But 476 x 365 =	173,740 days
Add (14th March to 6th April, both inclusive)	24 days
Add for leap years	116 days
	173,880 days

And 69 weeks of prophetic years of 360 days (or 69 × 7 × 360) = 173,880 days.

It may be well here to offer two explanatory remarks; First, in reckoning years from BC to AD, one year must always be omitted—for it is obvious, *ex. gr.*, that from BC 1 to AD 1 was not two years, but one year. BC 1 ought to be described as BC 0, and it is so reckoned by astronomers, who would describe the historical date BC 445 as 444. . . . And secondly, the Julian year is 11m. 10. 46s., or about the 129th part of a day longer than the mean solar year. The Julian calendar, therefore, contains three leap years too many in four centuries, an error which had amounted to eleven days in AD 1752, when our English calendar was corrected by declaring the 3rd September to be the

Much there is of Holy Writ which unbelief may value and revere, while utterly refusing to accept it as Divine; but prophecy admits no half faith. The prediction of the "seventy weeks" was either a gross and impious imposture, or else it was in the fullest and strictest sense God-breathed ($\theta\varepsilon\acute{o}\pi\nu\varepsilon\upsilon\sigma\tau o\varsigma$, 2 Tim. 3:16). . . . To believe that the facts and figures here detailed amount to nothing more than happy coincidences involves a greater exercise of faith than that of the Christian who accepts the book of Daniel as divine. There is a point beyond which unbelief is impossible, and the mind in refusing truth must needs take refuge in a misbelief which is sheer credulity.

14th September, and by introducing the Gregorian reform which reckons three secular years out of four as common years: *ex. gr.*, 1700, 1800, and 1900 are common years, and 2000 is a leap year. "Old Christmas day" is still marked on our calendars, and observed in some localities, on the 6th of January, and to this day the calendar remains uncorrected in Russia.

Key to Story Titles

ABBE The Abbey Grange
BERY The Beryl Coronet
BLAC Black Peter
BLAN The Blanched Soldier
BLUE The Blue Carbuncle
BOSC The Boscombe Valley
BRUC The Bruce-Partington Plans
CARD The Cardboard Box
CHAS Charles Augustus Milverton
COPP The Copper Beeches
CREE The Creeping Man
CROO The Crooked Man
DANC The Dancing Men
DEVI The Devil's Foot
DYIN The Dying Detective
EMPT The Empty House
ENGR The Engineer's Thumb
FINA The Final Problem
FIVE The Five Orange Pips
GLOR The Gloria Scott
GOLD The Golden Pince-Nez
GREE The Greek Interpreter
HOUN The Hound of the Baskervilles
IDEN A Case of Identity
ILLU The Illustrious Client

LADY	The Disappearance of Lady Frances Carfax
LAST	His Last Bow
LION	The Lion's Mane
MAZA	The Mazarin Stone
MISS	The Missing Three-Quarter
MUSG	The Musgrave Ritual
NAVA	The Naval Treaty
NOBL	The Noble Bachelor
NORW	The Norwood Builder
PRIO	The Priory School Mystery
REDC	The Red Circle
REDH	The Red-Headed League
REIG	The Reigate Squire
RESI	The Resident Patient
RETI	The Retired Colourman
SCAN	A Scandal in Bohemia
SECO	The Second Stain
SHOS	Shoscombe Old Place
SIGN	The Sign of the Four
SILV	Silver Blaze
SIXN	The Six Napoleons
SOLI	The Solitary Cyclist
SPEC	The Speckled Band
STOC	The Stockbroker's Clerk
STUD	A Study in Scarlet
SUSS	The Sussex Vampire
THOR	The Problem of Thor Bridge

3GAB The Three Gables
3GAR The Three Garridebs
3STU The Three Students
TWIS The Man with the Twisted Lip
VEIL The Veiled Lodger
WIST Wisteria Lodge
YELL The Yellow Face

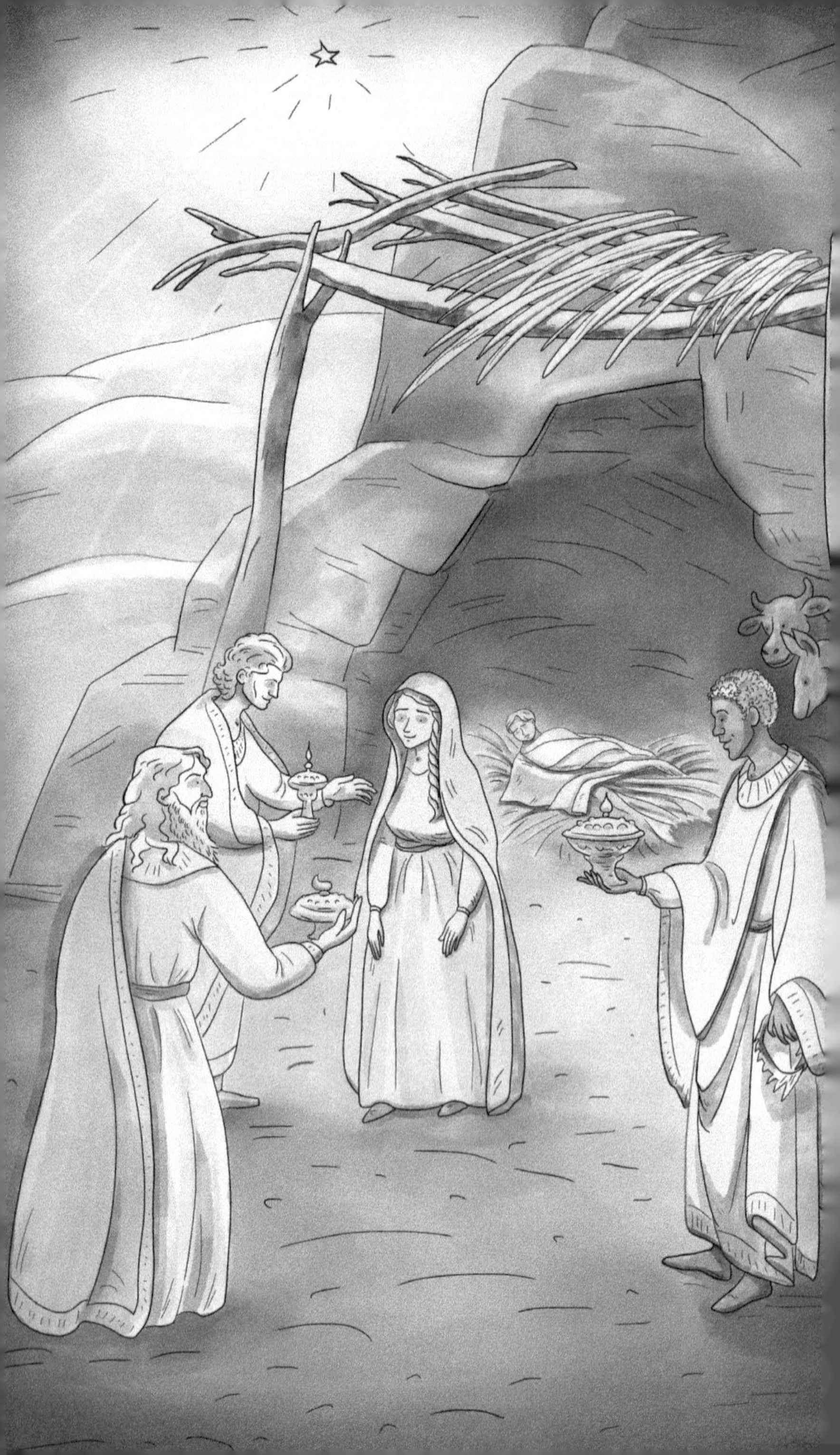

A Royal Visit

It is generally believed that the monastic library of the Saint Catherine's monastery on Mt. Sinai long ago revealed all its secrets. Surely, after Tischendorf's discovery and almost miraculous saving from the ignorant flames of what would be known as Codex Sinaiticus, *the Saint Catherine's manuscript collection has become little more than a touristic location? But as a matter of fact, this is not the case. During a brief scholarly sojourn there, I was shown a medieval Latin manuscript titled* Historia vera de Magis Novi Testamenti. *The following narrative, rendered here into colloquial English, represents the essence of that work.*

. . .

The youngest of the Magi was Balthasar of Ethiopia, a black Prince of kingly rank, from whose line would come Prester John, the greatest of the Christian sovereigns of Africa during the centuries following the collapse of the Roman Empire. Many important and ancient biblical manuscripts were to be found in the Abyssinian libraries, and tradition says that the Queen of Sheba, who brought gifts to King Solomon, was Ethiopian.

Not long after his twentieth birthday and just prior to the beginning of what we term the Christian era, Balthasar's learned advisors brought to him a scroll of the sacred writing of the prophet Daniel and demonstrated to him from that text a calculation as to the advent of the Divine Messiah.[1]

That event was soon to transpire, and the advisors recommended that Balthasar immediately prepare to make contact with other notables of like character and integrity, so as to plan appropriately for what would surely be a divine manifestation. They

---

1. See Sir Robert Anderson's classic, *The Coming Prince*, for a detailed discussion of Daniel's prophecy of the "seventy weeks" and its prophetic connection with the dates of our Lord's earthly life and ministry. —*M.*

were convinced that Melchior of Persia and Caspar of Tarsus were the ideal leaders to be consulted.

Balthasar agreed and soon set out on a journey that would have many unexpected consequences.

• • •

On reaching Melchior's court, Balthasar was amazed to find, if not Plato's "philosopher-king," a reasonable approximation. Melchior, a man of about 40 years, was not only a sage ruler but a Zoroastrian, learned in astrology—not the occult, predictive sort, but a scientific, observational concern with the movements of the heavenly bodies. Balthasar was especially impressed that Melchior strongly agreed with the biblical condemnations of astrological religiosity, whereby one could bypass human limits by predicting the future, known, in fact, only to God himself.

Melchior checked and rechecked the Daniel passages, and agreed enthusiastically that the dating corresponded with amazing specificity to their own time. And he informed Balthasar that there was every reason to believe that a remarkable conjunction of planetary bodies was soon to occur. Surely there must be more than a chance relationship between the biblical text and the heavenly phenomenon!

So the two Magi set forth together to discuss the entire matter with Caspar.

• • •

Casper, a Jewish convert, was exceedingly wealthy and was now a "royal" more in an economic sense than a political one. By the time of Balthasar's and Melchior's visit, he was of *troisième âge*, but in vigorous health. Though of royal blood, he had no choice but to accept Roman rule, and he stayed as far away from the political imbroglios of the time as he could. The Jews of Tarsus had gained many concessions that were eventually available to Jews throughout the Roman Empire. Tarsus functioned as an enviable city-state, with which the Apostle Paul would later identify himself as a citizen.

Caspar directed the attention of his visitors to Jerusalem, the center of the biblical world. Surely Messiah would appear there!

On agreeing with the two sovereigns as to the legitimacy—indeed, the immense importance—of their being present at the coming Messianic event, Caspar emphasized that it would be churlish not to bring gifts. Tarsus was one of the cities along the famed "silk route" by which luxury goods traveled from China to the Near East and ultimately to Europe, and Caspar was sure that appropriate gifts could be found in Tarsus before the three set out on the six-hundred kilometer journey from Tarsus to Jerusalem. Balthasar and Melchior settled on perfumes and spices of the highest quality, and Caspar himself simply took purest gold from his own coffers.

And so, having correlated Old Testament prophecy with the appearance of celestial phenomena, the three Magi set out for Jerusalem.

• • •

As the Gospel testimony relates, when the three arrived in Jerusalem, they went immediately to the court of the Jewish king Herod the Great to obtain more specific details of the Messianic appearance. Who better to provide such than the current "King of the Jews"? Herod's advisors were convinced that Bethlehem would be the divinely chosen location, basing their argument on the text of the prophet Micah: "But thou, Bethlehem Ephratah, though thou be little among the thousands of Judah, yet out of thee shall he come forth one who is to be ruler in Israel; whose goings forth have been from of old, from everlasting."

"Why didn't we know that?" said Melchior to Balthasar and Caspar. "We also had access to that text. In any event, let us indeed make our way to Bethlehem. And by the bye, isn't Herod's son Antipas called a 'fox'? Caspar may have been impressed by Herod's wealth, but I simply do not trust him."

· · ·

The three therefore proceeded to Bethlehem, guided by a miraculous point-of-light in the sky not far above them. During that short journey, the three revealed their personal expectations.

Balthasar: I look forward with intense anticipation to the rule of the true Messiah— who will banish once and for all two evils:

racism, and the lack of respect for our natural world.

How often have I observed the condescending glances of the whites who have come to my court—their whispers and veiled humor as they regard my people. The essence of Messiah's mission must be to eliminate all that and place all races on a plane of absolute equality.

Also, Messiah will bring about a new appreciation of Mother Earth. As long as we disregard our true homeland, we lose our true foundation and the one genuine heritage for our children. I agree with that Prince of Angleterre (wasn't his name Charlie?) who kissed Gaia and saw the land as a divine revelation.

Melchior: For me, the Messiah will validate the religious aspirations of all peoples. True, our Zoroastrianism does not teach the same message as the Jewish Scriptures—but genuine sincerity is surely present.

The Messiah will surely honor the grand variety of beliefs in our world and may even blend them all together to provide a world faith embracing all peoples!

How I long for that eventuality.

Caspar: I am more of a practical person than you two, and I am sure that the Messiah would agree with me. I am not interested in ideological theories. For me, it is a question of "seeing is believing." I can't visualize or make sense of philosophical ideas or conflicting religious viewpoints. Give me something concrete—and valuable: gold, for instance.

With gold, I can obtain whatever I really want. And I can purchase the thinkers and scholars and ancient manuscripts that will give me ideas that make me feel comfortable.

It is said that "of the making of books there is no end." Why should I accept one fellow's ideas over someone else's? I choose what works for me.

. . .

Inevitably, each of the Magi felt uncomfortable with the declarations of the other two.

Balthasar: But surely, Melchior, since the many religious views in existence contradict each other on the most fundamental level, no one of them could be true at the same time as the others? Didn't even the ancient Greeks recognize the law of noncontradiction? The

Messiah would certainly not repeal that essential law of thought. There would have to be a rejection of false ideas the moment the truth is revealed.

Caspar: I must agree. That is only common sense. But Balthasar, what is this environmental nonsense? Would there ever have been progress had we left "nature" as it is? And suppose we somehow maintain Mother Earth intact; will that have any profound effect on human nature? I believe that people will go on amassing wealth and privilege and power, as they always have done.

Melchior: Like Caspar, I am certainly not a racist. I believe that, whatever one's color, one's self-centeredness is exactly the same as that of others. Everyone wants to dominate in some area or other, and unless Messiah could change that, everything will remain just as it always has been.

But I find Caspar's rationalistic materialism hard to take. If possessing things were really all that important, why would we three be on this quest in the first place? We know full well that there must be something (Someone?) above and beyond this poor earth and its limited treasures, or life would simply not be worth the effort of living.

• • •

And lo, the three arrived at a humble stable in the presence of a maiden and a baby. Angels sang, "Glory to God in the highest, and on earth peace to men of goodwill." Shepherds were present, with their gifts of lambs.

As the three Magi knelt before the Christ child, Mary spoke:

You have come with your notions of what Messiah is to do. I have learned that it is best to say simply: "Behold, the handmaid of the Lord. Be it unto me according to thy word."

We have been told to name the child Jesus—"for he shall save his people from their sins." That must mean that Messiah comes to save. There may well be positive results beyond salvation: a reduction of racism, greater respect for our natural world, and the like. But the reason for this baby's advent is the transformation of human hearts—to show a fallen race its sin and to provide a ransom that will open the doors of heaven.

Your gifts are appropriate: gold for a King (not gold as an object of worship), the perfume of frankincense as recognition that you are in the presence of no less than Deity, and embalming myrrh because this little child will die for the sins of us all.

In sum, better that you should be silent in the baby's presence, jettison your preconceptions, and take him into your hearts.

• • •

As the Matthean text tells us, the three royals were led by a dream not to report back to Herod, but to return to their homes by another route. In that dream, they were also told not to publicize the details of their voyage, for "such information could be used by the Child's enemies, and your lands will later—in the fullness of time—be evangelized and opportunity given your peoples to accept or reject the wondrous gift you have been privileged to witness. The baby, grown to manhood, will declare: 'I am the Way, the Truth, and the Life: no one comes to the Father but by me,' and his chosen apostles will preach: 'There is none other name given among heaven by which one may be saved.'"

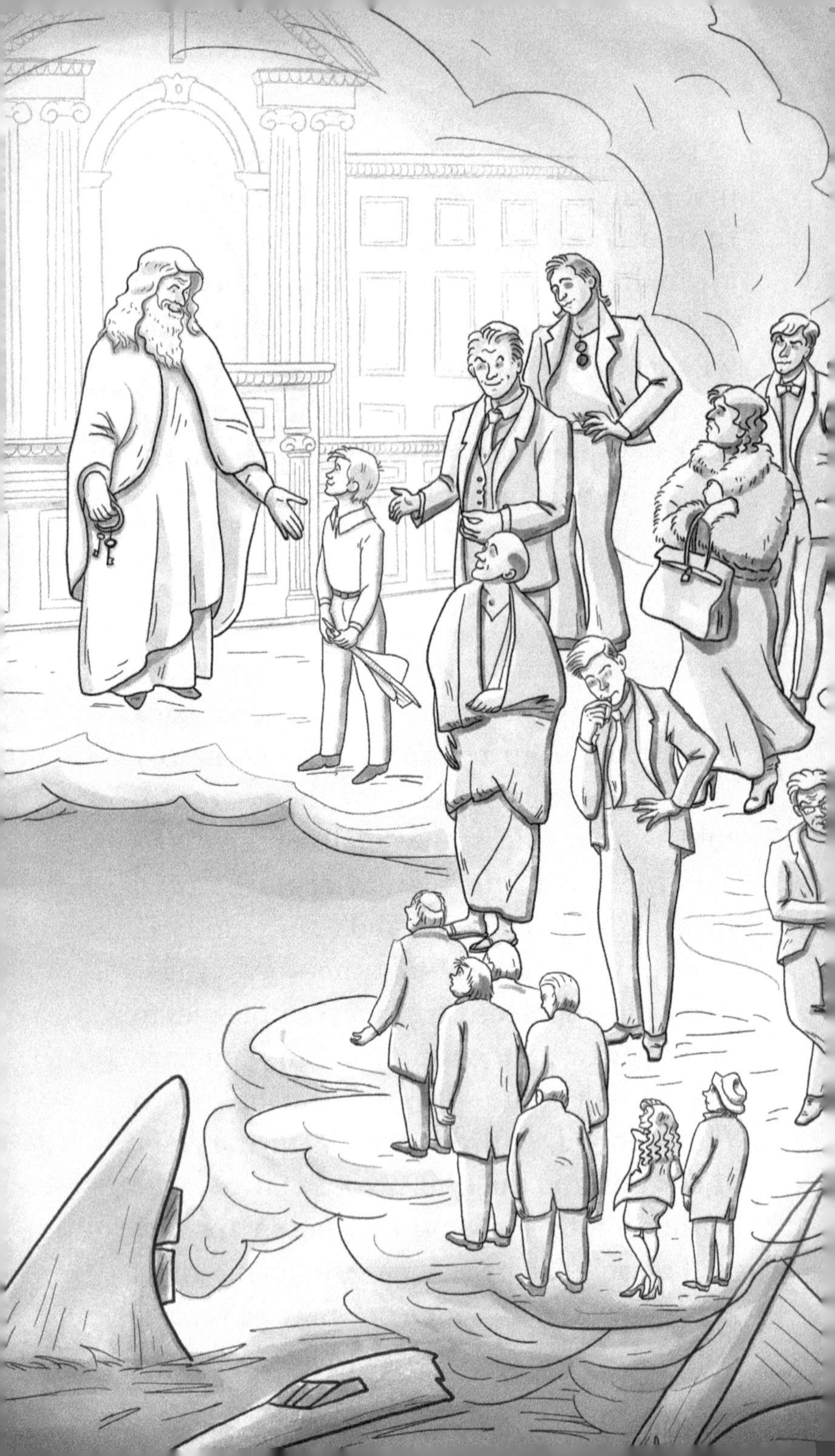

Judgment Eve

Prologue

I have been once again invited as a guest lecturer at the Reformed Theological University in Sárospatak, Hungary. This always provides the perfect excuse to visit the capital, Budapest. When in Budapest, I generally stay away from Pest and focus on historic Buda.

So here I am—in a small, medieval café close to the magnificent St. Stephen's Cathedral. It is the first week of Advent and the café is closing early. It will soon be five o'clock and no more customers will be allowed to enter, though those already there can stay as long as they wish. The sun has already set but the glorious facade of the cathedral is clearly visible through the bottled windows of the café.

I go to the bar to order another Tokaji, and when I return to my table, there is Walter Martin, ruddy as ever, sitting across from me. "Ah," says he, "I see that you are still partial to a fine Tokay wine, but it was always the Alsatian variety—the Pinot Gris—that turned you on."

When, with difficulty, I recovered my composure, I mumbled somewhat as follows. "Walter! How many times since your death I have needed to talk with you, and you never came. No one else that I have ever known could, as you effortlessly do, put his finger instantly on the real issue in a complex theological or personal problem. I have had to struggle so hard in your absence."

"You have to understand," Walter replied, "that we are very seldom allowed to return. You simply have to rely on the revelation God gave you in Holy Scripture. Heaven is not another Roman Catholic magisterium to tell you what the Bible is really saying. Let Scripture interpret itself."

"So," I interrupted, "why are you here now? To admit that you have finally discovered the value of infant baptism?"

"Not the reason, at all. Though I must say that my baptistic rationalism got quickly corrected in the next world. But to be sure, every theologian has some problematic areas in his or her world view—and that happens to apply to you, too!"

"So why have you come back? I have missed you terribly."

"We'll have plenty of time together in eternity. I'm here to give you a manuscript. You have written or edited a vast number of non-fiction books but only one fictional tale—the ghost story included in your Principalities and Powers. The editorial committee where I now operate has come to the conclusion that you need to do something fictional, to convey in a different way what you have been trying to get across in a more-or-less academic fashion."

"Walter, all my professional life I have assiduously avoided 'Christian fiction'—the kind of trashy stuff that fills the shelves of the evangelical bookstores. Please don't expect me, at this late stage of my career, to produce a fundamentalist cowboy novel or a soporific evangelical romance."

"Hardly, O Great One.[1] Our publications committee is far too sophisticated for that.

---

1. Not vanity. Walter always addressed me as such—never explaining why.

The manuscript I'm passing on to you is raw material for a novel in dialogue, along the lines, perhaps, of Chaucer's *Canterbury Tales* or Dante's *Divine Comedy*—to give your readers an idea of what may occur before each person experiences his or her personal last judgment. We are confident that you can pull this off. After all, look what you did to a host of debate opponents, such as Thomas Altizer and the death-of-goders. I still recall how you once polished off a Princeton Theological Seminary prof in the question period following your lecture there, under the larger-than-life portrait of the great B. B. Warfield."

"You are, as always, too kind. Reciprocally, I recall that national TV program where you appeared with a self-proclaimed practicing Christian homosexual. When he reproached you for not appreciating true same-sex love, you instantly responded with 'You mean, sticking it into the rear end of another man?' A bit crude, perhaps, but it made the point (so to speak) that a Christian must never take a position that contradicts biblical teaching."

"Ah, yes. I recall that program. Created quite a fuss with the network. But I always enjoyed making life difficult for media people whose god was generally political correctness.

"But time—in your world, not in mine—is slipping away. Take the manuscript with our compliments. Since you are convinced that French is the language of heaven, it's in the language of Molière. *Bonne chance et à bientôt* (*pas plus que vingt ans pour toi*). Au revoir."

And suddenly he was gone. A crumpled document stared up at me from the surface of the old wooden table.

1. The Scenario—Heaven

"Up there?" Once, in the question period following a public lecture at Cornell University, the eminent theologian Donald Grey Barnhouse of Tenth Presbyterian Church in Philadelphia was asked by a snotty student, "So you seriously think that heaven is a real place?" Barnhouse: "Right. X-miles from here."

*A magnificent courtroom,
with a fine judge's throne.*

St Peter to God Almighty: Really impressive. I especially like how well it invokes a nineteenth-century Gothic/Romantic feeling. It's definitely Burne-Jones.

God: We modeled it after the Royal Courts of Justice in London. But we've also assembled a modern courtroom, in Scandinavian IKEA style, though the angels had a terrible time putting it together from the kit. That one's for candidates who suffer from historical chauvinism and think that nothing is worth bothering with prior to the twentieth century. What's on today's agenda?

St-P: The Concorde air crash. A slew of candidates, most of them obviously well-off and well-educated, representing a variety of belief systems.

G: That crash is a real tragedy—and not the fault of the Concorde at all. Some careless mechanic at another airline left a metal part on the runway and it led to the loss of all those lives. And based on my omniscience, it will be the end of the Concorde—the most advanced aircraft humans have ever developed. Previously, the best everyday reminder of original sin seemed to be the fact that Jehovah's Witnesses wake people up early Saturday mornings, on the one day they have to sleep in; now, it may well be the Concorde disaster.

St-P: In any event, I'll need to interview the entire passenger list.

G: But as usual, the candidates can be grouped into categories, reducing the total from the 110-passenger capacity of the plane to a workable number?

St-P: Indeed. It would appear that some twenty interviews will handle the situation.

G: Good luck—or rather, God bless. Have your report on my desk by the end of the week.

2. The Child

St-P: You are our youngest arrival today. How old are you?

C: I'd be thirteen on my next birthday, but now, I guess I'll always be twelve.

St-P: Not necessarily, but we'll leave that one for another day. Were your parents also on the plane?

C: No. They traveled ahead by ship and were to meet me when the plane landed.

St-P: Do they go to church?

C: Christmas and Easter and once-in-a-while in between.

St-P: What do you like to do?

C: I love building model airplanes and robots. My first idea was to become an engineer.

St-P: You changed your mind?

C: I got to thinking about becoming a pastor. My grandmother got me into reading the Bible. I did a chart of those family trees in the Book of Genesis and then I began wondering where the story was going. In the New Testament, I got taken by Jesus. Don't know quite what happened, but everything changed. The leaves on the trees became brighter and things made sense.

St-P: What was it about Jesus that grabbed you?

C: Well, some people who heard him when he was on earth said that nobody ever spoke as he did. He taught me that though I am full of myself, there's a way out of that. He didn't have to die for me, but he did. I'm going to miss things down below, but he taught that the Kingdom of Heaven belongs to little kids like me. Can I see him now?

3. The Atheist

A: This is quite a surprise!

St-P: You didn't think you were going anywhere after death?

A: Definitely not. Death is the end. Period. The soul is nothing but an illusion, as is God the Freudian Father-figure, a projection of our longing for meaning in a cold, impersonal universe. All is material, and when the body dies, nothing of the person remains.

St-P: So what are you doing here?

A: I haven't worked that out yet. At the funeral of my fellow atheist, John Mortimer, the author of the Rumpole stories, the clergyperson said, "Won't he get a pleasant surprise."

St-P: I wonder why she thought the surprise would necessarily be a pleasant one.

A: You have a point there. The universe isn't as I wanted it to be.

St-P: That's not exactly what I meant. Were you not impressed by the evidence of the Transcendent by way of the Second Law of Thermodynamics, and the need for a cosmic intelligence to account for biological complexity, the human person, etc.? Didn't it bother you that, without God, no absolute account of moral values or human rights can even in principle exist, leaving humanity in the throes of relativism and totalitarianism (Pol Pot, Stalin, Hitler, and company)?

A: Ah, but there are always ways of getting around unpleasant academic arguments. As a lawyer, I saw that there are two sides to every question.

St-P: On the other hand, don't the tribunals have to come down finally on one side or the other, and don't they endeavor to do this according to the weight of evidence?

A: In theory, yes. But one doesn't always have to go with evidence one finds unpleasant. Take a recent argument by a former evangelical turned atheist. Refuting the necessity of a historical resurrection of Christ, he maintains that it is "quite plausible to suppose that either Joseph of Arimathea or some other third party removed Jesus' body from the tomb without the knowledge of the disciples and without them [sic] coming to know of the final resting place of the body" (James Fodor).

St-P: But surely, that argument is pure conjecture. There is no evidence whatever of a change of tombs—and had there been, the disciples would have been the people most concerned to know where the burial in fact took place. Perhaps something else is going on that makes such argumentation acceptable to you?

A: Well, now that you mention it, what has always bothered me about God and religion is that if all that were true, I would not be, in the words of the Invictus, "the master of my fate and the captain of my soul." I must be the Lord of my own life, not a slave to the will and values of some alleged cosmic power.

St-P: You have clearly identified the issue. The question is not whether there is a God; the theologian Paul Tillich (whom we here have trouble quoting positively very often) was right that there really are no atheists, since everybody has an "ultimate concern"—a god—of some sort. Even if it's not the true God—the God of the Bible—it will be a deity of some variety. Very often, it's the atheist himself or herself who thinks that he or she runs the universe by creating the only values that exist.

A: Right on! As Jean-Paul Sartre put it, "There are no omens in the world, and, if there were, we would give them their meaning." I am the sole source of values in a cosmic vacuum.

St-P: Well, as C. S. Lewis, one of our most quoted authors, has put it, no one is "sent" to hell. Hell is chosen by those who think they are god and resent the existence of a competing deity. Your destiny has always been in your own hands, and what you have sown you will be reaping—forever.

4. The President

St-P: Mr. President, what were you doing on that flight?

P: Good question. I should of course have taken the Presidential jet. But I wanted to show my constituency that I was just an average guy.

St-P: But considering the cost of a flight on the Concorde, that wasn't exactly what everyone could manage.

P: True, but it showed how important money really is. My example would encourage people to go after it as I have done my whole life.

St-P: Haven't you engaged in some pretty questionable financial transactions and hurt a considerable number of people as a consequence?

P: That's life. Some win and some lose. Isn't there a biblical passage or two referring to "the survival of the fittest" and "God helps those who help themselves"?

St-P: I don't think we are using the same Bible. The Bible we're familiar with here teaches that everyone is supposed to be his or her brother's keeper. Jesus talked about "the meek inheriting the earth." As a result of sinful self-centeredness, nobody gets saved through personal accomplishments. The only way to true life is to admit one's need and accept what God has done in Christ for a human race incapable of pulling itself up to heaven by its own bootstraps.

P: I never get into those rarified theological discussions. But that doesn't mean I'm not religious. My favorite preacher was Norman Vincent Peale. My whole life was based on his teaching of "positive thinking"—and see where this has gotten me!

St-P: Yes, yours is a very impressive résumé. But what is your view of personal sin? Your experience with the ladies is well known.

P: I don't think that "sin" is a category to be applied to me. We are living in a modern world, with modern morality. As a man, I like a little fun.

St-P: And if people get hurt?

P: So much the worse for them. The important thing is success. I am the living (whoops, dead) proof of that. By the way, when do the elections take place here? I intend to start preparing my campaign right away.

St-P: This is going to come as a shock, but we don't do elections here. The Head of State has always been in power and will always be in power. To use the biblical phraseology, he's the Alpha and the Omega, the Beginning and the End, the same, yesterday, today and forever.

P: This is really not my kind of place. There should always be room for improvement, and I am the person to achieve it. Are there alternative environments?

St-P: There is indeed one—where sin is not recognized and people eat each other.
P: Sounds like my kind of place. I've always been the eater, not the eatee. Au revoir.
St-P: I think you mean "Adieu."

5. The Rock Star

RS: Man, this is one impressive place!
St-P: Glad you like it. We've put a lot of time and effort into the built environment, especially our "many mansions" project.
RS: Any chance of my getting a chauffeur-driven Maserati up here?
St-P: Not really. We are into engineering perfection, and therefore, we are partial to the Citroën DS-23 Pallas with fuel injection and hydraulic suspension.
RS: But that's a car anyone could buy, at least when it was in production. I'm talking about a vehicle in a class where only the celebrated and filthy rich (like myself) could own one.
St-P: We've tried to be a bit more classless up here—though not in the Marxist sense.

RS: This courtroom could be turned into a super concert hall without a problem.

St-P: What would be the program? We generally feature Bach and Mendelssohn on our special occasions.

RS: That's fine for the stuffy crowd. But did they ever get audiences like mine? Thousands of screaming fans? I believe John Lennon remarked that the Beatles were more famous than Jesus Christ. At my funeral in Paris, the whole city will be weeping for the loss of its greatest star.

St-P: And what was your music's message?

RS: Love, man. When you feel it, go for it. Life is one passionate embrace after another—and not necessarily with the same partner. I've had a ton of relationships. Only problem is that with a diversity of heirs, there will inevitably be vicious fights over my inheritance.

St-P: Sounds like you have swallowed, hook, line, and sinker, the Greek idea of love: Eros. Love in that sense means getting all you can out of the other person—using the other as a ladder of passion to climb up to higher and higher levels.

RS: I was never into Greek philosophy, but that sounds just about right.

St-P: Actually, it's just about wrong. Nobody can love his or her way up to paradise. Humans are "dead in trespasses and sins," as the Good Book well puts it. The way up is to recognize that you can't pull yourself up. "No one has ascended into heaven but he who came down from heaven, even the Son of man who is in heaven"—to do for us what we can't do for ourselves. (Sorry, but I'm on a roll with biblical quotations at the moment.) Holy Scripture presents an entirely different idea of love: Agape, modeled on God's love for us: instead of seeking our own good, love descends to those in need, for their sake. That's the theme in most of Bach's music, so we're partial to it here.

RS: That's all good and well, I suppose. But just think about the sheer thrill and drama of my concerts . . . And those gorgeous, scantily clad backup singers . . . I was top dog for three generations of idolizing fans, and every one of them loved me. I made them happy.

St-P: Happy, yes. But joyous? Not hardly. You know that distinction? Happiness is temporary; joy is forever. Your succession of partners, for example, displays happiness: eventually, you tired of her or she of you, and a replacement was required. No concert of yours could be listened to forever without the audience going mad. I seem to remember a central American dictator who was finally flushed out of his secure retreat by the CIA's or the FBI's playing, night and day, rock music as loud as they could manage. Ultimately, the dictator couldn't stand another minute of it; even prison was preferable.

RS: I don't know if I would fit in here.

St-P: The issue isn't the style of the music. We have many contemporary musicians up here. The problem is the object of the music: is it God Almighty and his values, or the musician and his or her personal fame and fortune?

RS: That's a tough one. I've always been the center of my world.

St-P: There's only one place—and it's not here—where each inhabitant is his or her own god.

RS: I need to check that place out, and if it isn't up to my standards, I'll be back to you.

St-P: Sorry, no return fares are available. Between that place and here, there is a great gulf fixed, and no one passes from the one back to the other. Your life centered on yourself, so you need to go where that kind of existence is, sadly, normative. *Bonne (en effet, mauvaise) chance.*

6. The Advocate of Gender Theory

AG: Ah, heaven, where there is "neither marriage nor giving in marriage." I should find this right up my alley. Traditional marriage makes a sharp distinction between male and female. But we gender theorists go with Simone de Beauvoir who sagely declared: "You aren't born a woman; you become one."

St-P: What exactly does that mean?

AG: Simply that sex is not something biologically fixed. It's a social phenomenon. One doesn't have to be a male rather than a female, or a female rather than a male.

St-P: That would seem to have radical implications for society. As I recall, Simone de Beauvoir was the wife of the atheistic existentialist philosopher Jean-Paul Sartre, and they had a completely "open" marriage in which the two of them had many partners, both heterosexual and homosexual.

AG: Yes, that is consistent with gender theory. Traditional marriage is an outmoded concept. It just doesn't fit in the modern world. For that reason, we rejoiced at the success of the French *mariage pour tous* campaign and the US Supreme Court's Obergefell decision.

St-P: Logically, as the dissent pointed out in Obergefell, the next step may well be the legality of incestual and bigamous marriages. But most people do think in terms of normative marital unions.

AG: True. And so it follows that radical reeducation is a must.

St-P: Reeducation in what sense?

AG: The deconstruction of sex in the philosophical style of Jacques Derrida and Michel Foucault. As Hitler said, you must start with the very young if you want genuine change. In some elementary schools, teachers with a gender theory perspective have insisted that the boys wear dresses certain days of the week and play with dolls. The girls are given trains and fighter planes for their recreation.

The idea is to help the children to see that sexual differences are of no real significance. They can be a boy or a girl—whichever they wish.

St-P: I've also heard that there is a plan to eliminate separate bathroom facilities for men and women.

AG: Right. That's very important so that people of all ages will come to see the folly of placing males and females in airtight, separate compartments. This is particularly vital for women since the male-dominated, patriarchal society has limited their development, kept them from jobs open only to men, and paid them less than their male counterparts even when both are carrying out the same activities.

St-P: It doesn't seem to me that the only or best way to achieve "equal pay" is to obliterate sex distinctions, but I see how your argument is going. May I suggest some problems with gender theory?

AG: I suppose so. But I am sure that I have heard it all before.

St-P: First and foremost, if traditional marriage falls by the wayside, how will the race survive? Childbirth will still require the union of a man and a woman, and, without marriage, children will have no stable or principled upbringing. And if you say that the state will step in for the nurture of children, I'll have to remind you that the first generation of the Russian Revolution tried that, and the result was social chaos. Government and nurture don't really go together, since the fundamental function of the state is to keep people from eating each other, not creating a better value system. Secondly, there are genuine biological differences (some 6,500 genetic differences, as a matter of fact) between the sexes, so it is rather naïve to think that you can simply ignore them. Finally, there is a strange inconsistency in gender theory circles.

AG: What inconsistency? We are usually criticized for being too consistent.

St-P: The gender theorists we've observed are also invariably strong environmentalists. They are deeply concerned to preserve the future of the planet. But if the future is so important, and one demeans traditional sex distinctions and marriage, what will be the story in future generations? It would seem that those concerned with the future of the race would be the last ones to imperil the generations who will be coming on the scene later.

AG: Like most revolutionaries, we don't see our task as solving future problems. We correct a fundamental evil in the present and future generations will have to solve their own problems.

St-P: And finally, there do happen to be built-in structures in the universe, marriage and family being prime examples. God Almighty has made this crystal clear in both the Old Testament and the New: "God created man in his image, in the image of God created he him; male and female created he them." "For this cause shall a man leave his father and mother and shall be joined unto his wife, and the two shall become one flesh." Just suppose that is in fact true. Where does that leave gender theory?

AG: Well, of course, the two positions are simply incompatible. Isn't there a place I can go where my viewpoint will prevail?

St-P: Assuredly. There, all fixed distinctions are broken down and anarchy is raised to the maximum. It's the ideal location for revolutionaries who either think there is no God or that there are as many gods as there are revolutionary ideologies.

7. First Interlude: The Postmodern Buffet

St-P: Hello, all of you. Since quite a number of today's candidates identify themselves as postmodernists, we have set up this buffet for you. We know that you will enjoy it, even if it is the only treat we are able to offer before you may well decide to go elsewhere.

PM1: Very gracious of you. Before we sample the attractive selection of food and drink you have kindly made available, can we have a little talk?

St-P: I was hoping that you would want to converse a bit.

PM1: You seem to have a fairly rigid understanding of reality here, and the Bible reflects that. It suggests that, for example, there is only one right way of looking at things.

St-P: Yes, that is certainly the perspective of the Almighty.

PM2: And such rigidity is grounded, no doubt, in a correspondence view of truth—that only those assertions that correspond to a fixed external reality are "true."

St-P: You are very perceptive. We also hold to the law of noncontradiction, that A cannot be non-A under the same conditions and at the very same time.

PM3: That certainly reduces the scope of your universe.

St-P: True. But what other kind of universe would make any sense?

PM1: Let's see. Tell me your story, and I'll tell you mine.

St-P: Our story is very straightforward. The Almighty, out of love, brought creatures into existence; they consciously violated God's will and destroyed a future relationship with him; instead of leaving them to the just results of their *lese-majesté*, the Almighty himself took on the task of their salvation: he sent his only Son to die in their place; those who trust in him will live forever in his presence; eventually, the cosmos will be restored to its original, pristine condition.

PM1: That's really touching and personally moving. Now my story: Humans have infinite potential and, with serious effort, can produce a perfect world. Scientific progress is powerful evidence of this. But to achieve this glorious end, we must give up primitive superstitions, such as belief in a Deus ex machina who will solve the problems we should ourselves have solved but haven't.

St-P: These two stories don't seem to be compatible. They can't both be true.

PM3: And why not? Our story is as good as your story.

St-P: By what criterion?

PM3: By the fact that it is our story. If you don't accept its value for us, and thus its truth, you don't accept us as genuine persons.

St-P: I'm not sure that's the case. But the buffet table awaits . . .

PM2: Ah, good old American toasted cheese sandwiches: my favorite. And an excellent California Chablis.

PM3: Actually, I see these as Scandinavian open-faced anchovy sandwiches, and the wine is an Alsatian Pinot Blanc.

PM2: You stick with your story and I'll stick with mine.

PM1: My fellow postmodernists are going a bit far here. Of course, those two stories can't both be correct, but in the religious sphere, it's different. We can't allow one world view to dominate the vast number of others. Each person deserves his or her own truth.

St-P: Looks as if you are putting a wedge between ordinary life and theology. In the biblical view, "theological truth" operates in the ordinary, real world. God sends his Son into our human sphere as a true human individual. Jesus demonstrates his deity by miraculous acts in ordinary situations (water into wine—neither Chablis nor Pinot Blanc, however—at an ordinary wedding), dies on a historical cross, and rises again to ordinary proof (a doubter touches the hands and side of the crucified, now resurrected Jesus), and he makes a public ascent into heaven in the presence of ordinary human witnesses.

PM1: But if we were to go that route, we would have to believe that all philosophies and religious viewpoints contrary to yours are in fact false—at least at the

Judgment Eve 133

points where they contradict your story. That, in turn, would mean that honest believers in other world views can manifest falsehood—that some, maybe many, stories can be false.

St-P: Sadly, yes. Examples of such egregious false stories include the Nazi belief in racial supremacy, leading to the horrors of Dachau and Buchenwald, and the mass executions under a Stalin committed to the inevitable progress of materialistic Marxism.

PM2: I'm feeling a bit unwell. I think that I am having an attack of indigestion.

St-P: Actually, those sandwiches are *truffled pâté de foie gras d'oie* and the wine is a rarity from the Loire valley. Maybe one should first investigate what is really taking place and then stick with that reality.

PM1: We have always preferred a world that we can mold in our preferred direction.

St-P: There is a place where that is indeed possible, but it isn't here, and the food doesn't compare with ours. Stomach trouble is the order of the day. The train for that location will be leaving shortly, and one-way tickets are always available. Last I heard, the ticket price is just one's soul.

8. The Buddhist

B: I really expected another reincarnation. Becoming a cumquat or a three-toed sloth would have been particularly interesting. But apparently, my holiness of life has finally brought me to Nirvana.

St-P: This will doubtless come as a shock, but where you are is definitely not Nirvana. Anyway, if you had been absorbed into the totality of Being like a drop of water returning to the ocean from which it came, or like the candle flame returning to the Sun as its source, how would you have had the consciousness to know it? Your individuality would have ceased to exist as such.

B: True, true. The suddenness of all this has made me lose my sense of cosmic order and utter tranquility.

St-P: Another thing. Nobody stays here who thinks that his or her personal holiness is sufficient to gain eternal life.

B: Surely that cannot be so. That would contradict our Four Noble Truths and the Noble Eightfold Path.

St-P: We showed your Theravada—your Eightfold Path—to our Ethics Committee, and they concluded that its ambiguity paralleled that of the Boy Scout Oath and Law. Maybe it's not strange that there were Buddhist kamikaze suicide pilots in the Second World War.

B: Yes, but the strength of the Eightfold Path rests in its capacity for varied interpretations by each believer.

St-P: Somebody once said that an assertion or command able to mean anything actually means nothing.

B: I make it a point never to get into critical discussions; they disturb universal tranquility. The Four Noble Truths, however, are at the very heart of true enlightenment and the path to Nirvana.

St-P: The core teaching of those Truths seems to be the two axioms that "All life is suffering" and "The source of all suffering is desire"—leading to the conclusion that "To avoid suffering, one must forego all desire."

B: Exactly. This discovery led to Gautama's enlightenment and to his becoming the Buddha, the Enlightened One.

St-P: I note that those "Truths" do not limit the source of suffering to bad desires, but to desires in general.

B: Quite so. Desire is a mark of individuality, and one must pass into the realm of universal Oneness. Have you not read works by Christmas Humphreys, the eminent English judge who became a Buddhist convert and helped many westerners to move from their primitive religious ideas to something far more satisfying?

St-P: We have some of his books in our comprehensive bibliographical archive, but the author has preferred to reside elsewhere. If all desire is to be avoided, it would appear that distinguishing good motives from bad would be impossible—indeed superfluous even if possible. Could this perhaps explain the almost complete absence of any social ethics in Buddhist contexts? Wasn't it Gandhi who admitted, even though he was not himself a Christian believer, that it was Christianity, not the Eastern religions, that taught him the evils of the caste system?

B: The caste system—for that matter, all social structures—are epiphenomena, not the concern the true seeker of Enlightenment.

St-P: Evidently. Another question: if all desire, both good and bad, is to be eschewed, mustn't that necessarily also include the desire to become a Buddhist, the desire for enlightenment and Nirvana?

B: We are not troubled by seeming logical contradictions.

St-P: As I recall, the novelist Arthur Koestler, author of *Darkness at Noon*, after years of disenchantment with Marxism, went on a pilgrimage to drink at the founts of Eastern wisdom (*The Lotus and the Robot*). He was taken by mule back to a guru in a cave, and during the time with her, she said nothing to him but instead picked her toenail. On the way back, the monk who had brought Koestler to the guru, noting Koestler's discouragement, said, "She was telling you something." Koestler never figured out what, and ultimately the Koestlers, husband and wife, committed suicide.

B: A tragedy. He should have dug deeper, to discover real Meaning.

St-P: Just suppose "discovery" is not actually possible—or needed. As self-centered people, the human race must realize its incapacity to discover ultimates unaided and the necessity of being taught the difference between good desires and bad ones. Without that knowledge, one violates the will of God Almighty in one's own interests. A nonambiguous revelation from the Divine is the only answer. There is more than adequate evidence that God saw our plight and dealt with it himself on the Cross, and that he has given a clear revelation of himself in Holy Scripture. Not a confusing Tripitaka but an account of salvation that is historically and personally verifiable. Individuality then turns out not to be a sin; the sin consists of the individual putting himself or herself at the center of the universe and thinking that with enough cosmic huffing and puffing, one can arrive at a personal enlightenment. In reality, enlightenment comes (like everything truly good) as a gift, not as an attainment. The work is done by God—the only One capable of doing it—not by ourselves. "If anyone is in Christ, he is a new creature: old things are passed away; behold, all things are become new." (Sorry for the preaching; occasionally I get carried away . . .)

B: Don't apologize. But I really need to go where Christmas Humphreys is doubtless instructing others on the true path. I don't want to miss a reabsorption into True Being. I've struggled too hard, meditated too long, to forego that.

9. The Muslim

M: What a shame that I could not have arrived here as a jihadi martyr. As is, there probably won't be a single virgin assigned to me.

St-P: Well, that being the case, what are your expectations?

M: Holy Qur'an does not give us much detail on the next world. It appears to be a kind of oasis. Trouble is that I have never really liked dates (that is, dates as food). Allah is a God of sovereignty and predestination who expects his people to submit to his will. Except among the mystical Sufi, love doesn't much enter into the equation. I think that here I'd be happiest among the Calvinists.

St-P: A personal faith in Jesus is the only way to enter here.

M: No problem. The Qur'an regards Jesus as the greatest of the prophets before the coming of Mohammed. Jesus will be the judge of mankind at the end of the world.

St-P: As I recall, however, the Qur'an is quite definite that Allah cannot have a Son and that the Christian Trinity is not a true teaching.

M: Right. But there are Christian theologians who deny the Trinity also. Take David Jenkins, the former Bishop of Durham.

St-P: Yes, he was quite a problem. We sent lightning down onto his cathedral three days after his consecration to point out our lack of enthusiasm for him. The Jesus of the New Testament, however, clearly teaches Trinitarian faith. Jesus commands us to baptize in the one name of the Father, Son, and Holy Spirit. Jesus declares: "He who has seen me has seen God the Father." He sends the Holy Spirit as "another Comforter"—and the Greek word used for "another" there is "allos"—another of the same kind qualitatively as Jesus himself—compare the allotropic forms of sulfur—different appearances, but in every case sulfur. (Sorry, I sometimes get carried away with the original Greek text. I am especially concerned that people realize that Jesus didn't found his church on me, Peter. My name in Greek means a little stone, and he founded the church on a petra, the massive stone foundation of himself. But I digress.)

M: It should be obvious that the disciples misunderstood what Jesus was really teaching.

St-P: And how do you know that?

M: Because, otherwise, Jesus would not be the person described in the Holy Qur'an.

St-P: Let's see if I have heard you rightly. You are saying that if there is an apparent contradiction between what the eyewitnesses to Jesus' ministry say about Jesus, and what the Qur'an writes about Jesus at least six centuries later, the Qur'an, and not the New Testament, is correct?

M: But of course. The Qur'an is Allah's final revelation to mankind.

St-P: What makes you think so?

M: Because "there is one God, Allah, and Mohammed is his Prophet."

St-P: Do I sense a bit of circular reasoning here?

M: Why should that bother you? I am told that that is how the Calvinist presuppositionalists reason—and what about those evangelicals who say: "I believe in Jesus because the Bible says so, and I believe in the Bible because Jesus says so"?

St-P: In reality, Christians don't have to go that route at all. The New Testament documents can be shown to be sound simply as historical documents, and the eyewitnesses in those documents are innocent unless proven guilty. Had they falsified the life of Jesus, the religious opposition, being present during Jesus' life and ministry, would surely have blown the whistle on them. And Christianity triumphed in the Roman Empire because of Jesus' conquest of death by way of his resurrection, witnessed by many sane and sober people. Once you discover that Jesus was indeed the person he claimed to be—God come to earth—you have every reason to believe that the Bible is the very written word of God and fully trustworthy, for that is what Jesus himself taught.

M: But if that were so, my whole religious position would be wrong.

St-P: Not if it gave you a longing to meet the real Jesus—as it has for many Muslims.
M: You mean that I can actually meet him?
St-P: Indeed, yes—but on his terms, not yours. You need to be willing to accept him as he really is—not as your religion, or, indeed, as any religion would like him to be. And by the way, forget about those virgins . . .

10. The Christian Scientist

St-P: Good day, Madam.
CS: I've had better. As a faithful member of the Christian Science Church, and as a lifetime subscriber to the *Christian Science Monitor*, I have always regarded death as an illusion—like sickness.
St-P: Your practitioners have always told the faithful that a proper understanding of evil would show that it really does not exist.
CS: Exactly. We learn this from Mary Baker Eddy's wonderful book, *Science and Health with Key to the Scriptures*.
St-P: Hasn't that been shown to having been copied largely from the work of one Phineas Quimby, an itinerant magnetizer,

mesmerist, and ideological father of the New Thought movement?

CS: Mrs. Eddy was indeed a patient of Quimby and benefitted from Quimby's insights, but truth is truth, whatever the source.

St-P: True enough, but up here we've always felt uncomfortable with plagiarism. Martin Luther King Jr. was a leader of the civil rights movement, but we are much embarrassed by his doctoral dissertation, containing all sorts of material cribbed from other sources without acknowledgement. However, I digress. What does *Science and Health* teach? I ask because when we've strolled by those Christian Science Reading Rooms and looked at the window display with a Bible open to a passage and, next to it, *Science and Health* open to a page supposedly explaining what the Bible is saying, there never seems to be any connection between the two.

CS: You need to approach the subject with an open mind. Mrs. Eddy puts our central truth very succinctly: "God is Mind, and God is infinite; hence all is Mind." Christian Science teaches that evil, including all forms of illness, is an illusion. Our practitioners do all in their power to persuade the faithful to view the world as does the divine Mind and live in that confidence.

St-P: There have been legal cases where Christian Science parents have tried to refuse medical treatment for their sick children, and the courts have generally overridden the parents' wishes in the children's best interests.

CS: Very sad. We agree with many in the home school movement that the state must never oppose parental interests. The family is the core of society.

St-P: True enough. But a parent can surely abrogate his or her parental role, to the detriment of the child. That's sin, and a particularly egregious example of it. Our Lord said of those that maltreat little children that it would be better if a millstone were put around their necks and they were cast into the sea.

CS: We Christian Scientists have a real problem with what you call sin. Since sin is illusory, no redemption from it is needed.

St-P: So how does Jesus fit into your scheme of things?

CS: Here's one of the best statements of our view: "We acknowledge that the crucifixion of Jesus and his resurrection served to uplift faith to understand eternal Life, even the allness of Soul, Spirit, and the nothingness of matter." Jesus is our great model and example. We need to be like him—the kindly Man from Nazareth.

St-P: But how can you follow him if you don't accept his teachings, for example, what he says about sin, death as a result of sin, and hell as the consequence of refusing his salvation?

CS: We don't have to take the Bible literally.

St-P: That's clear, and it probably explains why *Science and Health* hasn't helped much in figuring out what Bible passages really mean.

CS: Mrs. Eddy, as a patient of Quimby, rightly saw that illness is a product of the mind. We must not be deceived by superficial literalism; we must attain higher levels of true spirituality.

St-P: Which reminds me of the story of the Christian Scientist who was stuck by a pin and remarked, "I shall admit this: the illusion of pain was almost as bad as the pain would have been."

CS: She had the right idea—and Ideas, not Material things, are what the cosmos is all about.

St-P: Christian Science in recent years has suffered tremendous membership declines, hasn't it? Indeed, now there seem to be a disproportionate number of elderly women as members.

CS: Yes, that is sadly true. But our churches are heavily endowed, and we widows of successful businessmen keep the torch lit. My dear, late husband, though not a Christian Scientist, left me an inheritance that made my Concorde flight possible.

St-P: Thank you for confirming some of our suspicions. When I hear "Christian Science" as the name of your church, I am reminded of Voltaire's comment about the "Holy Roman Empire"—that the name was a misnomer since that political entity was neither holy, nor Roman, nor an empire. Naturally, you won't want to spend eternity here, since you would regard it as illusory. The other choice will be more of an education for you—its reality being appallingly evident. Mrs. Eddy—and

Professor Quimby—will be there to fill you in on the details.

11. The Bishop of a Mainline Church

St-P: You must be The Reverend X.

BM: The proper title is "The Most Reverend X."

St-P: Sorry. I'll be more careful in the future. Tell me about your denomination.

BM: Wherever we have a local church, it is THE church in the community—representing the money, the leadership, and the highest levels sociologically.

St-P: I think that an appendix in Whyte's *The Organization Man* informs us that in New York City when a businessman becomes a vice-president of his corporation or the equivalent, he often changes churches—from Presbyterian to Episcopalian. Where do your clergy receive their training?

BM: Either in our own historic theological schools or at the very best universities here and abroad. We are especially partial to the German faculties of theology; they are at the progressive cutting-edge.

St-P: Indeed. I believe that in Germany, almost all the theological departments are part of the state system and are not controlled at all by the churches. It is not uncommon even to find atheistic professors of theology there.

BM: True. But that doesn't bother us. After all, we fully approve of modern biblical criticism; our practical theological disciplines always assume the accepted results of JEPD theory and *Formgeschichtliche Methode*.

St-P: How do you understand those "accepted results"?

BM: Simply that the biblical materials are not the product of the traditional authors but, rather, the work of later editors who rather clumsily pasted together a variety of documentary sources to give the impression of single authorship. Naturally, such materials cannot be treated as if they recorded reliable historical information.

St-P: But doesn't that eliminate any revelational quality that would justify there being a foundation of religious truth?

BM: Not at all. What's important is the ethical, moral teaching in the biblical books.

Granted, the old social gospel movement was a bit naïve, but they were on target that Christianity is a social movement. Our task is to transform society on the basis of new ethical perceptions: pro-choice abortion, homosexual relationships, right-to-die, genetic manipulation—to mention only a sampling of our positive concerns. The rather primitive biblical materials are a useful source of moral illustration along these lines.

St-P: I rather doubt that for the concerns you are promoting, you'll find much biblical illustration. But doesn't it bother you that not a single pre-editorial biblical "source" has ever been discovered? The earliest Old Testament manuscript we have is the Dead Sea scroll Isaiah, and that contains no breaks in the text that would suggest later editorial paste-ups.

BM: No problem. We identify the use of editorial subdocuments by a literary examination of the books as we have them. Stylistic changes, variations in vocabulary, sudden transitions in logic, etc., show us that later editors have been at work.

St-P: So it's a question of subjective literary judgment? The modern biblical critic says, in effect, if I had written this, I wouldn't have changed wording or argument that way, and so it follows that several earlier writers produced the grist for a later editor's mill. I recall somewhere that those skeptical of higher critical methodology have used it to show that James Joyce could not have written both *Ulysses* and *The Portrait of an Artist as a Young Man* and that Goethe could not have written part two of his *Faust*. Maybe God didn't choose your higher critics to write the Bible because God wanted to do it (to quote Frank Sinatra) his way. I am also impressed that Jesus himself apparently believed that the Old Testament documents were sound history, the product of divine revelation.

BM: Of course he did. But he was a product of his times. All the Jews believed that in his day.

St-P: But didn't he present himself as the divine Messiah—God come to earth to save mankind by giving his life a ransom for many?

BM: Yes, but such a claim was part of the limitation—the kenosis—he experienced in becoming human. Albert Schweitzer wrote his MD thesis to show that Jesus could believe he was divine and still be sane.

St-P: I believe the English translation contains a preface by a former president of the American Psychiatric Association who says that, in his experience, those in psychiatric wards who think they are God are definitely in the right place. But do not Jesus' miracles, and especially his resurrection from the dead, show that he was indeed the incarnate God—validating his views of the Bible (and of everything else he taught, for that matter)?

BM: Moderns do not go along with miracles. Since the eighteenth-century Enlightenment, we have come to a scientific, naturalistic understanding of the world. Physical law is unalterable.

St-P: I thought Einsteinian relativity had trumped Newtonian absolutism. As a matter of fact, Kepler and Newton believed the Bible; those laws of planetary motion were absolutized by others.

BM: In any case, it's the moral lessons in the Bible that are important for societal transformation. Take the story of Jesus' miraculous multiplication of the loaves and the fishes. The crowd was selfish and didn't share their food as they should have done. We preach the story to move our congregations to good works. And we especially stress the teaching of the Sermon on the Mount.

St-P: Wasn't it G. K. Chesterton who pointed out the inconsistency of the religious liberal who rejects the Virgin Birth because it is only recorded in two Gospels, Matthew and Luke, but loves the Sermon on the Mount, which is recorded only in—Matthew and Luke? Incidentally, how are the attendance figures in your mainline denomination?

BM: Not so good. We lose members every year, and fairly consistently in all parts of the country. But by our ecumenical unions with other mainline churches, the statistics still look impressive.

St-P: Most Reverend X, we wish that we could invite you in, but you would be miserable here. You would discover that God Almighty really is the author of a Bible that is revelatory and truthful from cover to cover; that Jesus, though a human in all points, was without sin, performed real miracles, and is the only way into the

Father's presence; and that the theme of his Sermon on the Mount is the truth that humans are not "perfect as their heavenly Father is perfect"—so that the Cross is the only solution (Matt. 5:48; Rom. 6:23). In contrast with your perspective, societies get saved only as the people in them find new life in Christ. Bye-bye.

12. The Pastor of the Church of Perfectly Correct Doctrine

St-P: Welcome!

PP: In a little book of traditional French clerical stories, there is the pastor, who, on being greeted by St Peter after the pastor's death, asked to be received by Jesus himself. On Jesus' arrival, the pastor declared, *"J'ai bien connu Monsieur votre père"* (I am well acquainted with your Father). Of course, that is just a story, but I myself really expected a more impressive reception.

St-P: I understand your frustration, but don't be offended. We are rather egalitarian in our procedures.

PP: Surely there is special credit for being doctrinally sound?

St-P: Let's put it another way: there are special sanctions for not holding to full biblical teaching.

PP: Our church body has always maintained that the purpose of the church is doctrinal purity, and I have endeavored assiduously to uphold that principle in every congregation I have served.

St-P: How have you achieved this in practice?

PP: We have cooperated with no other church bodies at all, and we have never engaged in any compromising common worship services, prayer meetings, or civic activities with those who differ with us in doctrine. It goes without saying that we have stayed strictly away from all those Billy Graham evangelistic campaigns.

St-P: Just out of curiosity, how did you happen to take this Concorde flight? Wasn't it terribly expensive for someone on a pastor's salary?

PP: My congregation gave it to me as a gift for the fiftieth anniversary of my ordination. We have, thank God, a few very wealthy members; for them, it's a family tradition.

St-P: How wonderful for you! But back to the issue of right doctrine. You say that the congregations you have served have engaged in zero cooperation with others, even with genuinely Christian bodies.

PP: Precisely. For example, a dreadful tornado struck the community where my current congregation is located. We refused to participate in the memorial service, even though it was not at all a worship character. Another example: lack of proper garbage collection has plagued our community for years, but we have not joined the protest marches—after all, Roman Catholics and even Buddhists were among the protesters.

St-P: I can fully understand your not engaging in any common worship with unbelievers or religionists of denominations who deviate from your church's confessions, but how do you justify no cooperation when the activity is not of a worship character?

PP: Ah, that's easy to explain and justify. If we were to cooperate, that would be saying that our faith does not penetrate all aspects of our lives. But since it does, we cannot work with others of no beliefs or deviant beliefs, since that would be saying that total truth is unimportant to us.

St-P: But isn't that the equivalent of Mennonite/Amish total separation from the rest of the world? Why do you not refuse to use zippers or drive automobiles that are not painted black?

PP: No, no. You do not understand. We are not against modern culture or new inventions. We believe that these can be the legitimate gifts of the Creator to our world. But we must never imply religious agreement when none exists.

St-P: Yet where the cooperation does not depend on a religious tenet, why is there still a problem?

PP: As I said, every act is religious, so we must radically limit all cooperation. Indeed, we have recently extended our position to multilevel separation.

St-P: What exactly is that?

PP: We began by separating from those who themselves deviate from correct doctrine. Then we moved—consistently— to separate from those who, though their own doctrine was not in question, were willing to cooperate with those of unsound beliefs. Recently, we have moved to a position of even greater consistency, in that now we do not cooperate even with those who, though they do not tolerate believers who refuse to separate from others as they should, cooperate with churches who are in fellowship with still other churches that refuse to engage in proper separation.

St-P: How have you handled catechetical instruction and the rite of confirmation?

PP: Two years of instruction, largely memorization of our denominational materials, and then confirmation—always at age twelve.

St-P: How do you know that each young person has actually confirmed—by personal commitment and genuine faith—his or her relationship with Christ? Doesn't this happen at different times in the case of the individual children? Do you counsel each child one-on-one?

PP: No. We have not fallen into *Schwärmerei*. One cannot look into the human heart. We stay away from personal issues with the confirmands.

St-P: Do the young people generally attend church regularly after their confirmation?

PP: That, frankly, has always been a problem; they don't. We attribute this to the secular climate of our day. But after all, they were all baptized.

St-P: Do you regard infant baptism as a kind of insurance policy for eternity? Doesn't Scripture contain a number of instances of former believers' falling away from their prior faith?

PP: Yes; we are "not once saved, always saved" Calvinists. But in Jesus' parable of the sower, only a small percentage of the seed ends up bearing any permanent fruit. And ours is a hopelessly secular world, with tremendous media pressures and intellectual objections to the faith.

St-P: Well then, does apologetics—presenting the evidences for the truth of Christianity—figure into your teaching ministry?

PP: Definitely not. Preaching the word is entirely sufficient. Old and young must simply accept God's truth and ignore the objections a pagan society throws up against it.

St-P: How large is your current congregation? Has it grown in baptized and confirmed membership over the years?

PP: We currently have 40 members and regular Sunday attendance stands at about 25. The congregation once had over a hundred members, but there has been, sadly, a steady decline—doubtless owing to the secular pressures of our pagan society.

St-P: Perhaps, but there just might be other factors in play. What do you see as the fundamental purpose of the church?

PP: Obviously, it is to create and sustain a community of sound belief.

St-P: Really? I thought that it was to "preach the gospel to every creature." Though the Scripture does indeed require consistency of belief in a church body, surely our Lord made the Great Commission the foundational principle of every Christian community? And if we allow ourselves to descend to a general policy of noncooperation, even when doctrine is not at issue, how will we ever carry out any kind of comprehensive evangelism to a fallen world?

PP: But we do that. Our church is open to all every Sunday (except, of course, for Holy Communion, which can be received only by members of congregations in our

Judgment Eve ≈ 161

denomination). And we include a listing of our divine services in the local paper. (We have, however, begun to wonder if that listing, on the same page as the church times of other denominations, might give the impression that we regard them as legitimate ecclesiastical bodies. Should that be the case, we would naturally have to cease our church's listings.)

St-P: In the interim, whatever your decision as to the local paper, it would appear that the world outside your congregation is going to hell in a handbasket, without much restraint from those who are called to do something about it.

PP: But, at least, our fidelity cannot be questioned . . .

13. Second Interlude: The Denominational Steering Committee

St-P: Because you gentlemen are so close, we have decided to interview you together.

All: What is going to happen to our church now? We go to an international meeting and end up here. Why did we not get individual air tickets on different flights, to ensure the survival of our beloved denomination?

St-P: I wouldn't worry too much about the future of your church. Frankly, no one is indispensable, particularly in church administration. But tell me about your ecclesiastical philosophy. The President of the Church should start this off. Then the rest of you chime in—Educational Director, Denominational Publisher, and Archival Historian.

CP: Our church must always be presented as the ideal. Negative criticism is out. For example, there is an independent journalist who continually brings up failures in our operation. That sort of thing must be crushed. The laity need to have absolute confidence in what we are doing.

AH: But there was that messy doctrinal conflict a generation ago when most of the faculty of our major seminary marched out to start a new theological operation that would have permitted radical criticism of the Bible. And more recently, our cutting-edge professor of intelligent design was found to hold an unfortunate position on the Great Flood of Noah, and we had to pressure him to resign.

DP: Well, all that is past history. The important thing is to ignore such events: never mention them in official church publications, pretend they never happened.

AH: Makes sense. But doesn't this smack of rewriting the past—as the early Marxists did by removing entirely the Beria article from the Great Soviet Encyclopedia?

DP: We are not writing a comprehensive history of the church—or doing history at all. We are cultivating believers who need to be fully satisfied with their church membership and who will contribute generously to its future. Of course, we sanitize all our official publications—to give the laity the conviction that ours is the perfect church for them. As for that journalist the President mentioned a moment ago, our publishing policy is to refuse any submission by an author who says anything nice about the fellow. And we try to excise references to those unfortunate doctrinal controversies that have occurred in our church circles from time to time.

AH: Seems odd that we are doing this. The official Confessions of our church all contain both "thesis" and "antithesis"—the latter being refutations of the false positions of heretics, not a few of whom were doing their thing within the church.

CP: Those times are not ours. In our secular age, the church must appear as a "mighty fortress"—one whose walls are never breached.

St-P: How do you see the work of your church colleges and theological seminaries?

ED: First, the seminaries. We are careful not to require uncomfortable defining of terms when we do our doctrinal examinations of potential faculty members. The important thing is that they sign on the dotted line and have prestigious backgrounds that will impress mainline seminaries and the accrediting agencies. Recently, we had a prof whose views were causing a disturbance beyond the seminary walls—and just at the time of a major financial campaign to raise funds! We eased him out. He received a "promotion" to a position outside our church entirely. And the contract of the prof who blew the whistle on him was not renewed—even though that prof had more degrees and publications than any other member of the faculty and received the highest possible "Rate your Professor" score from his students. For us, the important thing is not some kind of intellectual or theological attainment, or even the quality of teaching, but fidelity to the greater goals of the institution.

St-P: What about your universities and colleges—where students prepare both for church and nonchurch careers?

ED: In his interview to become president of one of our major universities, the winning candidate emphasized that he was "not an elitist." That gave him the presidency. We have never gone to the trouble of obtaining significant endowments; our schools are tuition driven. That means that the key lies in student numbers—warm bodies that will pay the freight. Of course, this has had implications for enrollment criteria and curricula choices. We stress, not classical subjects such as ancient languages with small enrollments, but more "practical" areas—veterinary science, nurses training, education, sociology, etc. We are gratified to see the proportion of students outside our church body grow constantly in comparison with the number of enrollees from our denomination.

St-P: But doesn't this reveal that your educational institutions are becoming indistinguishable from secular universities and colleges?

CP: Not at all. We conduct voluntary chapel services and have wonderful, thoroughly liturgical commencement ceremonies!

AH: Again, this does seem a rather different philosophy than what we find in the early church. St. Paul, as I recall, preached and defended the gospel to Stoic and Epicurean philosophers on the Areopagus—the intellectual center of Athens. I believe one of the converts became the first bishop of Athens. And St Paul focused his ministry on the major cities of the ancient world—to impact the climate of opinion of the day. From there, the gospel spread out into less influential areas.

CP: But that was another age. Our institutions can hardly compete with the Ivy League.

St-P: Certainty not when there is no effort even to try. God help the visible church . . . Our Lord had every reason to ask the rhetorical question, "When the Son of man comes, shall he find faith on the earth?"

14. The Television Evangelist

TE: Blessings on you, my son.

St-P: And good day to you. But I am not your son.

TE: A figure of speech. I use them a lot in my nationally and internationally broadcast programs.

St-P: Yes, we've noticed that when we've chanced on the networks that carry your evangelistic services. But frankly, that isn't often; it usually occurs when we can't find reruns of *Gunsmoke*.

TE: Well, you need to stay with our programming. Faith is in constant evolution: new presentation techniques almost every day. Now we're into podcasts and the social media.

St-P: How wonderful for you.

TE: You can't imagine! Why, just before the Concorde flight, I turned in my personal executive jet for the latest model—with widescreen television, a full bar, and three stewardesses. We keep two pilots on full pay all the time.

St-P: We've heard some rumors about your contacts with stewardesses.

TE: A man of my stature, under the kind of media pressures I face every day, needs a bit of release once in a while.

St-P: We'll not pursue just now your methods of gaining release. With a state-of-the-art private jet at your beck and call, why did you bother with the Concorde?

TE: The time factor. I needed to record virtually back-to-back in Paris and in New York. Going transatlantic in my jet would have taken too long. Time is money!

St-P: Do you think that you are building a church?

TE: In a very real sense, yes. Granted, we are unable to administer sacraments, but that's not at the very center of things in most traditional churches anyway. Preaching defines the church. And man, can I preach! We have our virtual congregations touch the screens of their TV sets to confirm their newfound faith.

St-P: What do you preach?

TE: I almost always start with something humorous and a bit of autobiography.

This relaxes the audience, and they love to hear about me so that they can identify with me.

St-P: And then?

TE: We get to the heart of things, the reason their lives are not perfect. They face illness, job dissatisfaction or loss, family conflicts, constant money problems. Why? Lack of faith.

St-P: And how can they get the faith they need?

TE: They need to believe God loves them, regardless of any peccadillos they may have committed.

St-P: But where will the faith come from?

TE: They've got to believe in themselves, their potential as children of God. That's the sure road to success and happiness. Look at me, as proof of the pudding! Have I not been a rousing success? They must of course show the reality of their newfound faith by contributing to my ministry. Tithing is the biblical way to do it. They can make commitments by credit card or even PayPal. Their generosity will be returned to them multifold by the Good Lord. The widow's mite is a start, but the more one gives, the more one shall receive.

St-P: Did you ever come across the New Testament teaching that "faith comes by hearing and hearing by the word of God"?

TE: Sure. They listen to me, and they get faith.

St-P: So hearing you is equivalent to hearing the word of God?

TE: Couldn't have put it better myself.

St-P: What do expect in heaven?

TE: Well, obviously, a mansion worthy of my spiritual accomplishments. And the opportunity to preach what I have always preached. There must be vast numbers even in heaven who would benefit from a deeper understanding of themselves and from the opportunities available to them.

St-P: There's a better place for you to preach that sort of thing. Where you will be going, everybody has always been trying to save themselves. They'll agree with you one hundred percent that repentance and grace have little or nothing to do with it. Those who have read the Bible quote texts out of context much as you have. You'll have a lot in common with them.

15. The Charismatic

HC: What an experience!

St-P: Yes. Death is quite an event—and best on just once occasion per person. The Second Death is to be avoided at all cost.

HC: I see my transformation as another miracle of the Spirit.

St-P: Well, the Holy Spirit really appreciates your confidence in him. At least you don't think he retired in the first century of the Christian era.

HC: Of course not. Revelation continues. In our churches, believers impart new revelations to the other faithful all the time.

St-P: Actually, just because the Holy Spirit is continuously active in history, it doesn't follow that revelation is open-ended. Jesus gave a special gift of the Spirit to the apostolic company (John 14 and 16), so that that they would remember everything he had taught them. The church then collected the writings of apostles and those who benefited from immediate contact with the apostolic band; those are the books that came to make up the New Testament.

HC: No problem. We have apostles in our church today.

St-P: You are using the term differently, and that's a real danger. The original apostolic company ended with the death of the last of the original apostles. We know that because, when Judas Iscariot was replaced, the replacement had to have been with Jesus from the beginning of his earthly ministry and a witness to his resurrection (Acts 1:21–23). The only exception was St Paul—"born out of due time," "grafted in," a unique apostle to the gentiles. Of course, no one else could be added after the death of the original apostles, since they alone had the gift of a comprehensive knowledge of Jesus' teachings so as to approve only proper additions to their company. Your "apostles" can't validate revelation or produce new biblical material in any sense of the term.

HC: I don't want to get into semantic arguments. The important thing is the continuing miraculous work of the Spirit—as manifested in tongue-speaking and healings. In our Pentecostal circles, one needs to have this kind of Second Blessing to be worthy of leadership.

St-P: I don't seem to find that requirement in Holy Writ. To be sure, the Spirit continues his miraculous work of healing. But since he "moves where he will," trying to institutionalize it, as at Lourdes or in your revival services, doesn't seem like a very good idea.

HC: You need to feel the Spirit's power in those glorious healing sessions! We are invariably moved to speak in spiritual languages. Then some of us, benefiting from the gift of interpretation, impart to the assembly the meaning of the revelation (perhaps you would prefer that I say, "inspiration").

St-P: You're learning. But this seems to elevate subjective feelings above biblical truth. We here have always appreciated Martin Luther's teaching that the entire gospel is *extra nos*—outside of us—not to be identified with our feelings, but with the objective work of God in judgment and in grace. Scripture seems to stress the Spirit's fundamental work as Advocacy—what we were talking about as that gift of "total recall" to the apostles that gave us the New Testament, and "convincing the world of sin, righteousness, and judgment"—i.e., the preaching of the Law—together with the Gospel by which people are saved. I suspect that the miraculous healing of Mrs. Slonk's ingrown toenail is somewhat less effective evangelistically.

HC: But our churches are growing, while others are doing just the opposite.

St-P: True enough. But I suspect that's due to your dynamism in door-to-door witness more than the tongues and the healings. Linguists, by the way, have pointed out that what passes for speaking in other tongues is actually not "language"—for which there are linguistic criteria never met in charismatic tongue-speaking, or, for that matter, on the day of Pentecost, when people miraculously spoke in actual languages they didn't know but that were understood by the native speakers of those tongues. The Pentecostal "interpretations" are really instances of independent preaching, and if they are not subjected to the test of biblical truth, they can constitute "another doctrine" than that revealed in the Bible. As for the impact of Charismatic evangelism, we praise God for it; it's about the only way, for example, that many aesthetically motivated, fundamentalist-hating Episcopalians ever moved away from liberal theology so as to get back to their original scriptural and doctrinal beliefs. But religion grounded in feelings will always be the house built upon sand, not on the solid rock of Christ's gospel.

HP: Well, at least we aren't the dead orthodox.

St-P: Thank God. But keep two things in mind. First, remind yourself of Jesus' story of that Pharisee who thanked God that he wasn't like that other fellow, the Publican. Second, though there is just one route to heaven, there are plenty of roads going the other way. Avoiding one error is no insurance policy against committing an equal but opposite error. As for you personally, here's the entrance code for the gate. You are really going to like the miracles we have available, and no offering plate has to be passed.

16. The High School Biology Teacher

HS: Well, at least now I won't have to worry about getting my teaching certificate renewed at the State Department of Education. Man, are those bureaucrats legalistic!

St-P: You taught biology. How did you handle the apparent conflict between Genesis and evolution?

HS: Easy. I avoided it entirely. Anyway, evolutionary theory is really far more than a theory: it's as close to scientific fact as one can get.

St-P: Really? I thought that fundamental to physics (the hardest of the "hard" sciences) is the Second Law of Thermodynamics that asserts the universal presence of entropy—that in any closed system the available energy moves inevitable to a condition of "heat death," or, in other words, the universe is running down. But evolutionary theory claims that, at least biologically, things are slowly but surely improving in the direction of greater complexity. The evolutionist sings autosuggestionist Emile Coué's optimistic mantra, "Every day, in every way, we are getting better and better." Thus pace the accepted view, mustn't biological evolution, even if true, have to be regarded just a minor, special case in a deteriorating universe?

HS: Don't ask me. I never messed with philosophy. My field is science education.

St-P: But you are teaching evolution as virtually scientific fact.

HS: Sure I am. All competent biologists accept it—not necessarily in a strictly Darwinian sense, but in the fundamental notion that living entities have developed naturalistically over millennia from simple to complex.

St-P: Ever read eminent scientists who disagree? For example, Nobel Prize winner Ernst Chain, Pierre Grasse in France, Sören Lovetrup in Sweden?

HS: Why should I read those people, distinguished as they may be? The School Board has made clear that evolution is the only position to be taught to the students. Any kind of special creation is out. The US court cases say the same thing. It's a First Amendment thing—separation of church and state.

St-P: Well, you are right about the court cases. They are very interesting. In spite of overwhelming efforts by experts in those cases to show the soundness of intelligent design on strictly scientific grounds, the judges have declared that to introduce any form of intelligence into the picture is to substitute religion for science. This seems very strange.

HS: Why strange?

St-P: We were always under the impression that scientific method meant that one needed to go with the facts wherever they lead. If the best explanation of biological phenomena turns out to be intelligent design, so what? Scientists are not supposed to prejudge the universe but endeavor to understand it, regardless of what the best explanation turns out to be.

HS: But in those cases, it was shown that some of the intelligent design people believed in God, were religious, and may well have been motivated by their faith to engage in scientific activity.

St-P: And so? Throughout the history of science, some of the greatest names have been Christians and motivated by their faith—Copernicus, Kepler, and a host of others. The issue shouldn't be why one chooses to do the research but whether the research is sound and the conclusions arrived at follow solidly from the data. Phosphorus was discovered in the seventeenth century by the alchemist Hennig Brand while boiling toads in urine: his motivations and personal philosophy are irrelevant; the result of his rather smelly activities was a valid and important discovery.

HS: All right. What do you think a proper educational approach should be?

St-P: Simple. Present the students with evolutionary theory, together with the best arguments for it and against it. Give intelligent design equal time. Let the students reach their own conclusions as to which explanation is the better one. At the very least, this would treat the students as mature adults, capable of making their own decisions, rather than objects for indoctrination.

HS: But I am still not convinced that there is any meaningful scientific case for intelligent design.

St-P: Here's just one illustration. One-celled animals such as the paramecium are amazingly complex; their system of cilia (like the oars of a boat by which they propel themselves around) has been compared to a sophisticated engineering operation—one requiring intelligent design.

HS: But that, obviously, is the product of naturalistic, evolutionary development—time plus mutation.

St-P: "Time" doesn't ever function as a causal factor per se; it just marks succession from point A to point B. And "mutation" is sudden, inexplicable biological change (it's just a word, not an explanation, like "instinct"). Most important, however, is that the one-celled beasties appear at the very beginning of the alleged evolutionary process. In other words, there hasn't been any prior opportunity for evolutionary development. One is at the first stage of things. Therefore, it follows, like the night the day, that there must have been an intelligence to program the one-celled animals with the complexity they demonstrate.

HS: Wish I had done a bit more study in this area. I'm a Christian believer, but I never put my faith and my science together. Had I done so, it could have been a real benefit to my students.

St-P: We here go for total integration of faith and knowledge. After all, the Boss made the stuff in the first place, and he's the most intelligent person we know.

17. Ms. None

MN: This is something else! I'm going to get my iPhone and take some shots. They'll be perfect with the European stuff I took during my holiday.

St-P: Actually, your iPhone disintegrated along with the Concorde.

MN: Yeah. I'm a bit disorganized after what happened.

St-P: You obviously like cathedral architecture. You're a churchgoer?

MN: Are you kidding? I'm neither a church member nor a churchgoer. In fact, I don't join any organizations. That's why they call millennials like me "nones." My own life is all I'm concerned with—and that's plenty enough to occupy my time. And I'm not the only one: I read a statistic recently that said that the number of Americans between eighteen and twenty-nine years old who don't do organized religion is four times greater now than it was thirty years ago. And Europe is now essentially a continent of nonchurchgoers.

St-P: What about the gospel of sin and redemption?

MN: A lot of malarkey, in my opinion. That's the kind of pious nonsense that I avoid by not getting involved in a church.

St-P: Come with me into our projection room. There's a film or two I want you to watch.

MN: Awesome! I love to binge-watch movies.

St-P: These, however, are more like home movies. I'm rather sure you wouldn't want others to watch them with you.

MN: Ah, I remember this. I used to do some significant shoplifting in that little boutique around the corner. Never got caught. The owner was pretty naïve—she really trusted me.

St-P: The store was the owner's whole life, and it operated on a very close margin. As a result of her losses, she had to close and ended up in bankruptcy. She's been institutionalized for chronic and apparently untreatable depression.

MN: Let's watch something else.

St-P: There you are with Jimmy.

MN: I dumped him not long after. He was too serious and not much fun in bed.

St-P: I think you told him you loved him.

MN: Sure, that's what I tell every guy I sleep with.

St-P: See what happened to him.

MN: Is that Jimmy? He's on drugs and has lost a great deal of weight. And he seems to be in some kind of relationship with that bearded biker.

St-P: Our information is that he really loved you and when you, as you say, "dumped him," he decided that no girl was trustworthy or worth it. He drowned himself in the soft stuff, went on to harder drugs, became a hopeless addict, and has concluded that he is really homosexual.

MN: But I had no way of knowing that things would turn out like that!

St-P: You were planning to go to law school, right? Have you ever heard of the criminal standard of "depraved indifference"? Here, we call that "sin."

MN begins to lose her smug composure; tears appear at the corners of her eyes.

St-P: Another question for you: Suppose someone, at great loss to himself, managed to pay all your outstanding debts, and also gave you a check for $100,000. Would you cash the cheque, or would you tear it up and throw it on the ground because you didn't believe there was sufficient money in his bank account?

MN: Of course I would cash the cheque, with my deepest thanks to the giver. To destroy the cheque would be like refusing to thank a lifeguard who saved you from drowning.

St-P: In the drowning scenario, would you say: "Good for me! I had the sense to grab onto the life preserver thrown to me." Or would you do everything you could to thank the lifeguard?

MN: The guard saved me; I didn't save myself. I have heard that there have even been cultures where, when this sort of thing happens, you then belong to the one who saved you.

St-P: We may be getting somewhere. In those churches you didn't attend (or at least in some of them that still believe the Bible), Christ is offered to you as the one who took all your depraved indifference on himself and canceled it out so that you could spend eternity here.

MN: I've been a real ass—and I've hurt so many people. I never realized any of this. Yes, it's my fault I didn't go to church, but no one ever told me what you've just said. Is there any way I can believe now?

St-P: If you never knowingly (with scienter) rejected this, and have heard it now for the first time as you stand on the knife-edge between time and eternity, the answer is perhaps yes. Our cardiologist will need to check the actual condition of your heart. His name is Jesus.

18. The Old Man

OM: What a relief that my transition was instantaneous—even though I could have used another glass of Moët & Chandon champagne before the crash. The last thing I wanted was a prolonged time of illness and pain. I just finished reading Alphonse Daudet's *Quarante ans de Paris*, where he ends with the account of the death of his dear friend Edmond de Goncourt. A real horror, especially for the family and friends.

St-P: Do you think these things just happen?

OM: There doesn't seem to be any plan. Why the Concorde? Why those particular passengers on it?

St-P: You are obviously a serious reader. Have you ever read Thornton Wilder? *The Bridge of San Luis Rey*—or his less known but much more profound novel *The Eighth Day*?

OM: I think I once went to a stage production of one of his plays, but it didn't move me particularly.

St-P: Well, the two novels I mentioned both deal with theodicy—whether there is divine action in history of whether it's all just, as Shakespeare's Macbeth put it, "a tale told by an idiot, full of sound and fury, signifying nothing."

OM: And what was Wilder's conclusion?

St-P: In *The Bridge of San Luis Rey*, a priest witnesses the sudden fall of a bridge in South America that has been there for centuries. Only a few people are on the bridge at that moment, so he attempts to "justify the ways of God to man" by investigating their lives, to discover precisely why they were the ones to die under those particular circumstances and at that particular time. He finds apparent reasons in some cases, but none in others. Ultimately, he is executed for heresy by the church authorities for his presumptiveness and hubris.

OM: And *The Eighth Day*?

St-P: Wilder narrates a complex family history, something like the Old Testament genealogies of people in the line from which Messiah will ultimately come, where no rationale for their individual lives seems to exist. Writes Wilder at one point: "The Bible is the story of a Messiah-bearing family, but it is only one Bible. There are many such families whose Bibles have not been written." And at the novel's end: "There is much talk of a design in the arras [tapestry]. Some are certain they see it. Some see what they have been told to see. Some remember that they saw it once but have lost it."

OM: What's your point?

St-P: Simply that the tapestry is too complex to be unraveled on earth, but that doesn't mean it doesn't exist. We have some great theodicy seminars here; you can sign up at the registration desk. For example, Job teaches a great course based on his book.

OM: But my own life? So much of it seemed utterly arbitrary.

St-P: Do you remember all those close shaves you've had in your car? The time on the interstate when you dozed off and were just missed by an eighteen-wheeler? How about when you had the wrong date in your calendar for that critical job interview and later discovered that the company was about to go into liquidation? And wasn't it strange how you sold those stocks of yours just before the market crashed?

OM: But what about all the messes I wasn't able to avoid—or even anticipate?

St-P: As I said, the tapestry is a very complex one. As Job's book makes clear, there are events that occur within cosmic struggles of which the participant may never be aware. The principle, in any event, is straightforward: "All things work together for good to them that love God" (Rom. 8:28). Observe, however, that (1) this is not a promise to unbelievers, and (2) it applies only to genuine believers in God, that is to say, those who have found God in Christ (Matt. 11:27; Luke 10:22). I have often been amazed that that verse is seldom used as an incentive to conversion in evangelistic preaching. One would think that having a real purpose, a meaningful life, and assured guidance would warrant serious consideration of the claims of Christ . . .

OM: I tell you, though, getting old has been no fun at all. I'd like to meet the authors of books with titles such as "Life Begins at Eighty." They always write that trash when they are much younger and haven't been spending most of their time with medical specialists or in retirement homes.

St-P: Can't argue with that. Sin has thoroughly messed up the human situation, and since "the wages of sin is death" one could hardly expect the years immediately preceding death to be devoid of problems.

OM: Another thing that bothers me in this connection is the biblical assertion that "Jesus was tempted in all points as we are, yet without sin." No problem with his being without sin, but he never grew old, so he couldn't have been tempted by the despair of old age—the thought that suicide might be the best way out—especially when one cannot any longer seem to accomplish anything, much less take care of one's family, and one has become a real burden to others.

St-P: Jesus' being tempted in all points as we are doesn't have to mean that he had every experience quantitatively that humans have—and he obviously didn't (for example, he was never a soldier or had to face the necessity of killing another human being). He was, however, fully tempted in the qualitative sense: he experienced, just as the human race does, the temptations of loneliness ("the Son of man has nowhere to lay his head"); grief over one's inability to keep others from destroying themselves ("How often I would have gathered you as a hen gathers her chicks, and you would not"); and stark despair ("My God, my God, why have you forsaken me?").

OM: Where is that seminar registration desk?

19. The Discouraged Pastor

DP: Well, that's that. The only thing I ever won was a free Concorde ticket—and then the plane crashes. A trivial ministry in a trivial place. Hardly enough money to live on and almost nothing to leave to my family. Thank goodness my wife is a nurse and will be able to find work now that I am gone.

St-P: I am getting the idea that you consider your pastoral career to have been a failure.

DP: That's putting it mildly. During my entire career, the flashier clergy passed me by on their way to cushy, urban pulpits or well-paid Synodical offices. They substituted guitars for the organ, repetitive gospel music for the classic hymns of the Reformation, and preached topical sermons featuring the latest news in the press and on television. I tried so hard to be faithful to our Confessions, for example, when some clergy downplayed personal holiness and disregarded the clear teaching of the Confessions on the Third (or Sanctifying) Use of the Law, I insisted that we maintain that biblical belief.

Result: I was ignored or treated smugly as a hopeless conservative.

St-P: I believe that you were also criticized for spending too much of the congregational budget on foreign missions rather than expanding the local church site with a gymnasium and state-of-the-art media equipment.

DP: Indeed. I never thought that the church was the buildings or the physical plant—much less the electronics. My fellow clergy could toss off a sermon in no time using PowerPoint. I struggled every week to study the biblical text in the original Greek or Hebrew and to explain it so that the congregation would hear God's word, not my personal opinions or the latest religious theories.

St-P: I recall that W. H. Auden somewhere said that, unlike most professional writers, he worked his head off to get his poetry exactly right. Of those facile writers, he said, "They have their reward."

DP: As for me, I don't see any reward at all. Not that I performed my ministry for personal gain—quite the opposite. I guess that I should have thought more of myself...

St-P: That would have been a great mistake. Come with me to the projection room. I want you to see a film or three featuring you.

DP: Not the media here! I thought that death would at least deliver me from that.

St-P: See that teenager? She was considering an abortion, followed perhaps by suicide. You convinced her that her unborn child was a person deserving of protection and love. Later she married very well, and her son became a medical scientist who discovered cures for some previously untreatable diseases. Thousands of lives were saved as a result.

DP: I had no idea. I don't even remember her name.

St-P: Maybe you'll remember this boy. He was a terror in your catechetical class—objecting to everything as being irrational. You spent hours with him, offering apologetic arguments that were unassailable and in language he could understand and relate to. He went on eventually to become a professor of philosophy at an Ivy League university. His books and scholarly articles have made him the American C. S. Lewis. There is no telling how many young pagans have come to the faith through his writings and lectures.

DP: I never imagined that my ministry would get beyond Podunk State Teachers College.

St-P: And here's a fascinating one. This fellow from a little African country dominated by Islam was a member of a refugee family your congregation befriended. With much difficulty, you persuaded the immigration people that the family had actually been members of a persecuted group at home and were not here for economic gain. You obtained housing and work for them and somehow managed a university scholarship for the boy. He earned a good degree in politics and government at returned to Ugubougu, eventually to become president of that little country. As a serious Christian believer, due to your solid preaching and teaching, he fought tenaciously for human rights in his homeland. Islamic influence was radically curtailed, women (who had not even been permitted to obtain drivers' licenses) got the vote, and that little country is now considered by experts to hold the key to a sea change in human rights throughout Africa.

DP: I'm not sure where even to find Ugubougu on the map.

St-P: That's not really important. What is significant is that we've mapped your ministry in detail. Well done, good and faithful servant. You have been faithful over a few things; we shall make you ruler over many things. Enter into the joy of your Lord.

20. Envoi

St-P: Well, that takes care of this lot. A mixed bag, as always, arriving from a world dead in trespasses and sins but illuminated by grace.

G: Things will look up considerably with the new heaven and the new earth.

St-P: You can't imagine how I long for that. I'm sick and tired of a creation always groaning and travailing.

G: Trust me. The new heaven and new earth are in the works and the timing has been meticulously worked out. But don't ask for more details. Only I have that piece of information—not even my Son is privy to it.

St-P: I think that's what bothers me most about the human condition is its stupidity—the fact that humans ignore or reject exactly what they need to live productive lives.

G: You mean the gospel.

St-P: Precisely. You have done absolutely everything for their salvation, even though they in no way deserved it. By sheer love and grace, you offer free salvation to anyone who will admit his or her need, take personal responsibility for contributing to the human mess, and accept the gift of eternal salvation obtained by your Son as a result of unimaginable suffering on his part. But what is their response? To try every which way to save themselves by further exhibitions of self-centered egotism. Has nobody ever learned the lesson of the Tower of Babel?

G: As I recall, it was George Santayana who sagely observed that "those who refuse to learn from history are forced to repeat its mistakes."

St-P: Indeed. But most of them don't even believe any longer that the biblical record is veridical history—in spite of your own Son's having declared, "If they do not believe Moses's words, how shall they believe my words?" And even a little honest observation of their own personal lives would lead even a half-wit to the same conclusion: No fallen creature or fallen society can build a tower to reach heaven. Add to that the fact that "every knee shall bow and every tongue confess that Jesus Christ is Lord." Instead of doing obeisance when it would do them some good, the fallen race waits until the Last Judgment to be forced to its knees—to its eternal loss.

G: Well, I've done all I can. Isn't it time for a wee repast—in anticipation of the coming Wedding Feast of the Lamb? Don't know about you, but I'm for *Crêpes Suzette au Grand Marnier*. The flames always remind me of that cosmic transformation on my calendar.

Epilogue

Well, there we have it. I fervently hope that Walter Martin and his heavenly committee will be satisfied.

Do such dialogues actually precede final judgment? Or does judgment occur instantaneously after death? No way of knowing until our personal judgment takes place.

But there are some certainties on which we can rely before that final event.

First, there is no transmigration of souls, no second chances, and no intermediate, purgatorial state: Hebrews 9:27.

Second, there are definitely not "many roads leading up the mountain to heavenly perfection." Only one path takes you to eternal bliss: John 14:6.

Third, heaven is not the only possible destination after this life; another (and dreadful) alternative exists: Mark 8:36, 9:43; Luke 16:19–31.

If your response is, "But that's the Christian answer, and we must approach this on a much broader religious or philosophical plane," recall that the issue is not particularism, but truth. If your doctor has a specific remedy for a specific disease, don't try to outsmart him by taking some other remedy that appeals to you more. He's the doctor; you're the patient. Reversing roles can be fatal.

Suppose you decide to question the doctor's qualifications and seek a second opinion? Problem is that only Christ, the Great Physician, has risen from the dead and is in a position, as the unique Son of God, to pronounce on the subjects of salvation and eternity.

Therefore, Reader, you might do well to go with the fiction at the root of this work. Pretend that you are yourself in the presence of the Lord of history and that it is time for your personal dialogue with Him. What will He ask you? What will you reply? What will be the eternal consequence?